Echo from
the past

Eli B. Toresen

Echo from the past

Originally published as: *Ekko fra fortiden*
Copyright © 2000 by Eli B. Toresen
Cover illustration: Stabenfeldt A/S

Translation: Studio Imago
Edited by Kathryn Cole

Printeed by AIT Trondheim, 2004
ISBN: 82-591-1148-9

Contents

Chapter 1
An attic full of secrets

"It's creepy up here!" Thirteen-year-old Lynn Roberts shivered as she looked around the huge dusty attic. It was gray and cloudy outside and the two skylights did very little to brighten the dim, dark attic. Two old-fashioned cast-iron lamps hung from beams under the roof, but even so they only lit a small part of the space. The chests and cases piled up in corners where the light couldn't reach, were vague, colorless shapes.

Lynn cautiously lifted the lid of a big chest that she could just barely see. It was full of old books, and it gave off a smell of dust and mildew. Lynn's nose started to itch and she quickly lowered the lid.

"This attic would be a perfect setting for a horror movie," she said, happy she wasn't alone. "I wouldn't be surprised if it was haunted."

"It is haunted," said Camilla, Lynn's cousin. Her voice sounded a little muffled because she was bent over a large trunk and was busily rummaging through its contents.

"There are tons of old clothes in here," she said enthusiastically. "Maybe we can try some on later."

Lynn, however, wasn't at all interested in old clothes. "What do you mean, it's haunted?" she asked, glancing over her shoulder as if she expected to see a ghost rattling its chains at any second. Lynn was surprised by her own reaction. She didn't believe in ghosts. After all, she was 13 and not a kid any more. When she was little it had been different. Terrified of ghost stories, she often couldn't sleep until her parents had looked under her bed or in the closet to make sure nothing was hiding there. Her brother was three years older, and merciless when he detected a weak spot. He'd never wasted an opportunity to tell her the most horrifying stories. He was particularly fond of a blood-curdling tale about a mystery rider who would break into the stables of naughty little girls and drown their favorite horses He'd only made up the story to tease Lynn, since she loved horses and had been taking riding lessons since she was seven.

Camilla's voice interrupted her thoughts. "I don't mean it's haunted up here," she explained. She shut the trunk and turned to face Lynn.

"The ghost's in the stable."

Lynn froze.

"Don't be scared! They say it only comes once every year or so," she added when she saw Lynn's reaction. "You'll get the whole story tonight. As far as I know, my mother is planning to tell the tragic tale of the estate to the guests after dinner." Camilla rolled her eyes. "I don't understand how anybody can be proud of a story that's so full of violence and misfortune. But you know how my mom is. She's always been interested in genealogy, and since she and Dad took over this place there's been no stopping her."

Lynn was curious, but Camilla wouldn't say anything more. "Wait till tonight!" she said. "Mom can tell the story better than I can, and I don't remember all the details."

Camilla wiped some dust from her sweater. "I look awful," she said, scowling at her clothes. "But who cares? We're only going to the stables, so I guess it doesn't matter if we're a mess. It is a good thing the horses don't care."

Lynn shook her head and chuckled to herself as she sized up Camilla. Camilla was not even 12 yet, but with her tall slim figure, long blond hair, and face that would make any model jealous, she appeared to be a couple of years older than Lynn.

Lynn sighed. She, on the other hand, was skinny and four inches shorter than her cousin. The dust had made stripes in her dark pants. One of her shoes was covered with cobwebs, and she was sure that her short, dark brown hair was too. By comparison, not a hair of Camilla's looked out of place. It had been like this forever. When they'd played together as little girls, Lynn was

9

always jumping in mud puddles and coming home filthy. "My little piglet," her mother called her. Camilla, her total opposite, usually came home as neat as when she'd left. How strange, thought Lynn. I just seem to attract dust and dirt, and somehow she repels it.

At the attic door, Camilla turned around and stuck her hand out towards the light switch, then brought it back. "Oh no," she said laughing. "We almost forgot what we came up here for. We were going to get that painting that we need to hang up in the entry hall."

The painting was right next to the door and was wrapped in a big pink sheet. "That sheet used to be white," said Camilla, seeing Lynn's surprise as she took in its unusual color. "But Dad was in a hurry once when he turned on the washing machine. He didn't realize there was still a pair of red socks in there with the whites. You should have seen his shirts!"

Lynn laughed. She knew how busy Uncle Thomas and Aunt Anne had been after they had moved to the old estate. They'd wanted to renovate it and turn it into a charming, cozy family hotel. Since the work wasn't completely finished, the hotel couldn't be officially opened, but they had five guests this evening, who had all read good things about it in the local paper.

"You can't start too soon with good advertising for the hotel," had been Thomas's response to Anne's protest that they should wait until everything was ready. "The entry hall is done, the kitchen is ready to go, the dining room is all furnished, and we have that grand old library. The guests can use that as a sitting room, since the living room still looks a little messy."

Camilla's mother had ultimately given in, and as a result, the Richmond Hotel was up and running. Lynn hoped it would go well. She had heard her parents discussing how risky it was to start a new business these days. But Aunt Anne and Uncle Thomas didn't seem to be too concerned, Hopefully, that meant there was nothing to worry about, Lynn thought to herself.

Carrying the huge, heavy painting downstairs, Lynn tripped over something soft and warm. It was Mephisto, Camilla's cat, who had silently made his way upstairs and was now winding around their legs. Lynn gave a start, her elbow hit the wall, and she nearly dropped the painting. Attempting to regain her balance, she stepped on Mephisto's toes and the cat howled in protest.

"That was close!" she laughed once she was firmly on her feet again. "Your mom would have just loved it if we'd damaged this painting."

She looked back over her shoulder. Mephisto was standing at the top of the stairs swinging his tail back and forth, looking insulted. He'd come up to the girls to be sweet and affectionate and had been stepped on for no good reason.

"He's grown so big!" said Lynn. "The last time I saw him he was tiny. Now he must weigh a ton."

Camilla laughed. "No wonder he's so heavy. He's a world champion kitchen scrap thief. I don't notice him growing because I see him every day. But maybe we should put him on a diet."

"Poor Mephisto!" giggled Lynn, visualizing the starving tomcat looking up from a dish full of lettuce and carrot slices. "A diet wouldn't do him any good, though. He'd just go hunting for mice. There must be more than enough around here."

"Mephisto hunting mice? You'll never believe it, but he's really afraid of mice. He's scared of anything small that moves. Birds, too, thank goodness. But right after we moved here, the neighbors' dog came around and Mephisto attacked him. A huge Labrador! The dog was scared to death and ran away and I haven't seen him since."

Lynn laughed. "So," she said to Mephisto, "you don't pick on anything smaller than you are. That's very fair of you. Never mind that your mean old owner calls you a scaredy-cat!"

Mephisto, who still was looking insulted, ignored her. He strode through the hall holding his tail in the air and disappeared from the girls' view.

∞∞∞∞

"This is Falcon," said Camilla, looking expectantly at Lynn. "What do you think?"

Lynn didn't answer right away. She was busy taking in the gorgeous Haflinger in the stall next to Camilla's horse, Silvana. Lynn still remembered how jealous she'd been when she'd heard that Camilla was moving to the countryside and would be getting her own horse. Lynn had wanted a horse of her own since she could remember, but her parents were completely closed to the idea.

"You can spend as much time with horses as you like at the riding school," her mother had said. "But getting your own horse is out of the question! The horse itself would be too expensive and then on top of that the board, feed, vet bills, and everything else would cost a fortune. Sorry, dear. Be glad we can afford to pay for your riding lessons and equipment."

Of course Lynn was happy about her riding lessons, but it would have been so different if she had had a horse that belonged only to her... Camilla was so lucky.

By contrast, Camilla hadn't even had to ask. Her father had suggested that since they were moving to the country where there were such good riding opportunities, they should buy a horse for her. And when Lynn wanted to stay with her cousin for the ten days of March break, he'd also suggested they arrange for a horse for her to ride while she was there.

Camilla phoned the day before Lynn arrived to tell her that her father had found a horse they could borrow from an acquaintance. Actually it belonged to his friend's daughter, but she would be away with some friends during the holiday. Besides, the daughter hadn't been riding much lately and the horse could use the exercise. The girl was happy to lend him, especially when she heard that Lynn had been riding since she was seven years old.

∞∞∞∞

"He's really sweet," said Lynn after a long pause. She'd been standing in the rain the entire time and hadn't noticed that the raindrops on her jacket were dripping down and making a little puddle around her riding boots. Quickly she took off the jacket and hung it on a hook inside the stable door. Then she slowly walked into the stall to greet the horse who was looking at her inquisitively from under his thick, pale forelock.

Lynn stroked Falcon's nose, then held her hands under his nostrils so he could sniff her and get accustomed to her smell. He lifted his head and blew warm air into her palms. It tickled. She ran her fingers through the long, full mane and then along his strong, golden back. Falcon stood still, seeming to enjoy the attention.

"Too bad it's such lousy weather outside," said Camilla. "It's no fun to go riding in this kind of wind and rain."

As if to illustrate her words, a strong gust of wind shook the roof. The old stable creaked and groaned, and a drawn-out, plaintive wail came from the hayloft. A shiver ran down Lynn's spine.

"Did you hear that?" she asked Camilla. "It sounded like someone groaning in pain."

"Oh no, it's just the wind," said Camilla firmly, but Lynn couldn't help noticing that her cousin shot a glance towards the hayloft, as if she were afraid that someone was up there in the semi-darkness, watching them.

Chapter 2
Family tragedy

The girls spent the rest of the afternoon taking care of the horses. Lynn reluctantly left Falcon's side to admire Camilla's horse. As the name indicated, Silvana was silver-gray, with a white mane and tail.

"Oh, she's so beautiful," Lynn said admiringly, but secretly she thought that Falcon was much more beautiful. His shiny coat gleamed like gold after he was brushed. "Do you know what breed she is? You forgot to tell me."

"She's a Swedish warmblood," answered Camilla,

stroking Silvana's belly with the brush. Silvana gave a start in fear and took a step back, then stamped the ground with her forefeet and neighed in protest.

Camilla gave her a calming caress. "She can't stand being tickled," she said to Lynn. "She always gives me trouble when I brush under her belly."

"Maybe I can distract her for you," Lynn offered. She stepped into Silvana's stall and started to talk to the horse as she scratched her forehead. It seemed to do the trick. Silvana relaxed visibly, and Camilla continued brushing her without difficulty.

∞◇∞

After dinner that night, everyone assembled in the library for coffee. But not everybody wanted coffee. Lynn and Camilla had gone to the kitchen and returned with sodas.

"I can't understand why anyone would drink coffee; it's so nasty and bitter," said Camilla making a face. She took a swallow of soda and turned her head to look at her parents and the five hotel guests who were sitting on the far side of the room.

One of the guests was a tall, slender man with a beard. His name was Arnold Stevens.

"He's staying here for two weeks, because he's giving a series of lectures at the university. He's an historian or something," Camilla whispered to Lynn.

Mr. Stevens's face was eager as he turned to Anne and said, "Mrs. Butler, I cannot wait another moment to hear you tell the story of the Richmond estate."

Anne opened her mouth to begin, but before she

16

could get a word out, a piercing female voice interrupted her.

"I'd just like to say that I've been looking forward to this all day! I just love stories. They're so amazingly interesting. Just think, what a unique opportunity this is to hear something about the recent past! I still remember, once when I was lodging in a hotel in England…"

Camilla gave Lynn a nudge. "Oh no! Chatty Kathy's going to take a turn," she complained. "I wonder if my mom will get a chance to say anything at all now."

The lady's real name was Ellen Andersen, but she had quickly earned the nickname Chatty Kathy from the girls. When Lynn arrived, Mrs. Andersen had been in the entrance hall. She had planted herself in front of Lynn for at least ten minutes, droning on to her in a high-pitched voice, talking a lot of nonsense about how nice it must be for sweet Camilla to have her even sweeter cousin visiting, but that they didn't look at all alike, although you could of course tell they were family, and on and on…

Camilla had tried to point out that their mothers were sisters, and the two girls resembled their fathers, but the babbling woman seemed not to hear. Eventually, the two had wished her a good afternoon and gone to Camilla's room, which they would share while Lynn visited.

Camilla glanced at the loud-mouthed lady and couldn't help giggling. With her garish yellow-green sweater and her teased-up hair, she looked like a parrot with makeup.

"You would think she'd talked more than enough during dinner," grumbled Camilla. "I don't see how she was able to get any food into her mouth. She rattled on non-stop."

"Yeah, and Mr. Stevens couldn't stand it, because he couldn't get a word in edgewise." Camilla shook her head as she listened to the constant stream of words flowing from Ellen Andersen.

"But he was not half as annoyed as, um, what's his name again..." Lynn discreetly pointed to a man who was staring at Chatty Kathy.

"His name is Dale, Oliver Dale," said Camilla. "Look at him! He looks as if he's about to explode."

She hadn't quite finished her last sentence, when Mr. Dale banged his fist on the table, rattling the coffee cups. He'd clearly lost his patience. In the silence that followed, he said, "Mrs. Andersen, I think I speak for everyone when I say that there's been enough chatting. We're all here this evening to hear a story about this estate, and now I'd like to hear what Mrs. Butler has to tell us."

He looked around as if expecting applause. He got it in the form of everyone nodding in assent, even the young couple, Eva and Daniel Arnesen. So far they'd stayed in the background, both during dinner and afterwards.

"They must be on a honeymoon," Camilla whispered in Lynn's ear. "I bet they can't afford an expensive trip to a resort, so they're staying here for a week in the country."

Lynn decided that the couple hadn't been very lucky in their timing, because it had poured all day. She hoped it would be nicer weather the next day, so she and Falcon could go out riding. Then she forgot all about

Falcon and riding for a while. Aunt Anne had begun her story. It was both thrilling and tragic.

"More than a hundred years ago, this estate belonged to a landowner, Alan Butler. His daughter Elvira was an extremely beautiful girl, and her father had great plans for her. Without her permission, he had promised her in marriage to the son of the gentleman who owned the farm next to theirs. This wealthy farmer was one of Butler's best friends. Since he only had the one son, nothing stood in the way of their joining these two huge properties.

"Elvira protested when she heard about her father's plans, but that made him angry. He called his daughter contrary and ungrateful, and made it clear that he would use any means necessary to force her into this marriage, which would give the family even more power and influence. Elvira's mother was no longer living, otherwise she might have taken her daughter's side, even if it hadn't helped. Alan Butler was stubborn as a mule and always had to have his way."

"Poor Elvira! What if you had a father like that?" Lynn whispered in horror to Camilla, who nodded in agreement.

"What the gentleman didn't know, however," continued Anne, "was that Elvira had already found the love of her life. It was the young Andrew Thorn, who did the accounting and purchasing for the estate. Knowing her father would never accept her marrying a young man with no fortune, Elvira kept her relationship with Andrew a secret. The two intended to travel west to California and start a new life together.

"They already had a plan. On the night of March 15,

Andrew would come to the stable to get Alivia, Elvira's favorite horse. Elvira was afraid that once her father found out she'd run away, he would take out his anger on the poor creature. Andrew was supposed to meet Elvira at their secret place in the woods. Then they would ride together to where a cousin of Andrew's lived and leave Alivia in his care. Of course, Elvira would have wanted to take the horse along with her, but it was too risky. Bringing Alivia would make them too easy to spot should Elvira's father decide to come looking for them."

Anne paused and took a sip of coffee. Everyone waited, anxious for her to continue. Lynn realized that her heart was racing with excitement. Would Elvira and Andrew escape from the clutches of this awful man?

"Alan Butler sensed that something fishy was going on," Anne continued. "And indeed, somehow he found out about his daughter's plan. On the very day she was going to run away, he flew into a rage and warned Elvira that she would always regret what she'd done. He locked her in her room and forbade the servants to let her out. Then he went to the stable to wait for Andrew to show up."

Anne ran her fingers through her hair and paused a moment before continuing.

"Elvira feared the worst. She knew how violent her father was. The only thing she could think of doing was to warn Andrew somehow. Quickly she wrote a letter to him, called one of the kitchen maids, and persuaded her to give the letter to Andrew.

"Her letter warned him not to come around the estate that evening, but to come to her the following night at their secret meeting place in the woods. How she would get there was another question, but she was hoping that her father would unlock her door once she promised to do anything he wanted. It might give her the chance to escape.

"But the maid never got an opportunity to hand over the letter," Anne said sorrowfully, bowing her head. "She was needed all day in the kitchen and couldn't even get to Elvira to tell her. So Andrew came to the stable as he'd promised. Just when he was about to lead the horse out, Alan Butler appeared with a gun and shot at him. Badly wounded, Andrew stumbled outside trying to get away from his attacker, but he got no farther than the woods behind the stable, where he collapsed and died. Alan Butler tried to follow Andrew to make sure he didn't get away, but he was prevented by Alivia. The horse must have been frightened by the gunshot. She kicked out, hitting Elvira's father on the head so hard that he lost consciousness. He was found later by the stable boy, who carried him into the house.

"Of course the servants told Elvira about the accident and let her out of her room. But no one knew about her father's crime and Andrew's fate. In her excitement the kitchen maid forgot to tell Elvira that she hadn't been able to give Andrew the letter. Elvira was counting on Andrew to be waiting for her in the woods as she had asked him to. Then they would get Alivia and flee together, before Alan Butler could recover and do anything to stop them.

"That evening, Elvira went to the woods to meet Andrew. But he never came, of course. She waited for hours and finally went home, stricken with grief.

"Elvira didn't get a wink of sleep that night, and when she got up the next morning, her nightmare continued," said Anne with a grimace. "The first shock was hearing that Alivia was dead. Elvira's father had regained consciousness and had ordered the poor animal to be killed immediately. Of course Elvira was shocked and heartbroken, but that was nothing compared with what was yet to come. Her father was confused and disoriented after the accident, but he proudly announced that he remembered shooting at Andrew and wounding him. Elvira sent a few servants to comb the woods and they found his body shortly afterwards. Elvira's father died the same day, probably from a stroke."

"That horrible man got just what he deserved!" cried Mrs. Andersen, who had been surprisingly quiet after Mr. Dale's reprimand. Horrible is putting it mildly, thought Lynn. That man was a monster. How could anybody treat his own daughter like that?

"After losing both her lover and her horse on the same day, Elvira never knew real happiness again," declared Anne gravely. "I'm sure she didn't miss her father too much. A cousin of hers took over the property. Elvira went into seclusion in her sorrow. She wasted away and died a few years after the tragedy."

∞∞◇∞∞

Anne looked around the circle. The room had gone completely silent. It seemed everybody had been moved by the tragic story.

Finally, Eva Arnesen laughed a little uncertainly and said, "Well, that sure beats any soap opera I've ever seen.

22

And people say 'the good old days' were so wonderful and peaceful!"

Anne smiled. "A lot happened back then that never came to light, I'm sure," she said. "People used to be able to keep scandals and tragedies a secret more easily. Today you see everything on television immediately."

"That cousin of Elvira's, who took over the estate – he was kind of a strange one, wasn't he?" remarked Thomas, reaching for his coffee cup.

Anne nodded. "Yes, he was pretty peculiar, all right. The only thing that interested him, besides running the farm, was collecting artworks and other objects. After he died, there was a rumor that he'd left a huge fortune behind. There were some vague references to it in his will. But it must have been just a rumor, because neither the family lawyer nor anyone else ever found a trace of any fortune. A few of the paintings were sold for a pretty good price, but it didn't really help the family out much. He'd probably overestimated the value of the paintings and other art objects, so the fortune existed only in his mind. Some of his collection is probably still here in the attic."

Anne laughed. "We've been so busy up to now that we still haven't had time to get a good look at what's up there. There are several chests and cases in the hayloft, too. It'll take a lot of work to sort everything out."

"Does that mean that you haven't given up on finding this supposed fortune?" asked Arnold Stevens.

Anne shook her head, smiling. "Frankly, I don't think we'll find a fortune," she answered. "So many people have looked for it and nothing's ever turned up. But I'm very interested in the Butler family history, and I've come across several references that lead me to believe

Elvira may have kept a diary. As soon as the hotel's completed and I have some time, I'm going to search through everything to see if I can find it."

"But what about the ghost?" Lynn blurted out.

Everyone stared at her in surprise. Lynn felt her face turn as red as a lobster and wanted to sink through a hole in the floor at that moment. Why hadn't she waited to ask about the ghost until she and Aunt Anne were alone? Now everybody would think she was terribly naïve. "I mean, of course I don't believe in ghosts or anything," she said, desperately trying to sound more grown up. "It's just that Camilla said the place is haunted…"

"That's true," confirmed Anne, "*if* you believe the local gossip."

She laughed at seeing Lynn's troubled expression. "No cause for alarm! Of course it isn't true. This place isn't haunted, but they do tell stories about a ghost that's supposed to hang around here. A couple of years after the horrible tragedy, a persistent rumor went around that Andrew had returned. They said he came in vain to the stable on the night of March 15, to fetch his beloved Elvira's horse. And now, the drama with the fatal shot repeats itself every year, so people say.

"They claim to see Elvira, too. She roams the woods in the place where she was supposed to meet Andrew…"

Anne fell silent and looked at Lynn and Camilla. She started to say something, but Thomas beat her to it.

"It all sounds scary, but you don't have to be afraid of anything," he assured the girls. "Ghosts only exist in people's imaginations."

"But we're not scared," said Camilla confidently. "We don't believe in ghosts, do we, Lynn?"

Lynn shook her head. "That's right!" she said unconvincingly. "But it was a really exciting story. I hope you find Elvira's diary, Aunt Anne."

The girls said good night to the guests and went upstairs. Mephisto followed close behind, meowing contentedly and rubbing against Camilla's legs. She picked him up and scratched behind his ears.

"Lynn's right," she said laughing, "you do weigh a ton." She put him back down and opened the door to her room. At the end of the hallway, in the dark, were the steps leading to the attic. When Lynn spotted them, an idea came to her.

"You know what?" she asked Camilla. "When we were up in the attic, I looked in a big chest full of books. Maybe Elvira's diary is in there. Wouldn't that be interesting?"

"Would it!" Camilla was wild with enthusiasm. "Come on! Let's look right now!"

"Now?" Lynn looked with dismay at the dark staircase. "There's no hurry, is there? Can't it wait until tomorrow?"

"Why wait? You aren't by any chance afraid of ghosts, are you?" Camilla teased.

"Of course not!" Lynn tried to sound as convincing as she could, but she got a bad feeling in the pit of her stomach at the mere thought of the enormous, deserted attic and its dark corners. Who knew what was hiding up there?

Reluctantly, she followed Camilla up the stairs. Apparently Lynn was too slow for Mephisto, because he slipped nimbly past her once Camilla had opened the attic door. It was hard to see in the dimly-lit room, but

25

Camilla was clearly not giving up before she had looked at every book in the chest. Lynn proved not to be much help, because she would look up almost every ten seconds to make sure nobody was peering over their shoulders. She had a creepy feeling that there was somebody there, but every time she whipped around she saw the same thing she'd seen a few seconds earlier. Her heart was pounding, and she was furious at herself for being so afraid. She envied Mephisto, who was calmly licking his paws. As she gazed at the handsome tomcat, he suddenly arched his back and looked right at a point in the middle of the room.

Lynn wondered what had gotten his attention, but she couldn't see anything special. Nothing moved or made a sound.

She gave a start when Camilla called out, "Got it!" in a triumphant voice.

Lynn had been so intent on trying to find out what Mephisto was staring at that for a second she had no idea what Camilla was talking about. Then she realized that Camilla had found Elvira's diary.

Lynn was just about to open her mouth and say something when Mephisto made a strange hissing noise. She looked at him. His ears were back and his hair was on end. His eyes were fixed on one spot. Suddenly he whirled around and disappeared like lightning through the attic door.

"Hey, what's the matter with him?" Camilla asked, surprised.

Lynn couldn't answer. She stood up, her eyes searching the attic for the slightest movement. The hairs at the back of her neck were standing up, just like Mephisto's had

26

been a minute ago. She had a terrible feeling that somebody was standing there in the dark watching them.

She jumped when she heard a creaking sound, as if
someone had stepped on a loose floorboard. "Come on!"
she called to Camilla, and ran down the stairs in panic.
She didn't even turn around until she was safe in
Camilla's well-lit room. But Camilla was nowhere to be
seen.

Chapter 3
Elvira's diary

"My mother's already hung the painting up," Camilla observed the next morning. The two had just finished breakfast and were on their way through the entrance hall and out the door.

Lynn, who was still embarrassed about her own reaction the previous night, was happy to talk about a safer subject.

She studied the painting, which featured a stream of colors flowing like a river in front of a dark gray background. Its heavy, old-fashioned wood frame made a pretty contrast with the modern painting. "It looks nice there," she commented.

"I'm glad you like it!" Anne had come out of the entry hall, but Lynn hadn't noticed her. "I did it a few months ago when I was taking a painting class. I found the frame in the attic, and I thought it was so pretty that I should find a use for it. The painting that was in it was so brown and depressing. I just masked the frame with tape and worked on top of the old painting. Not a bad job, if I do say so myself!"

Anne made her way to Arnold Stevens and Oliver Dale, who had just come into the entry hall. Camilla and Lynn didn't stop to say anything because they saw Chatty Kathy appear behind them, and they had no desire to get into a conversation with her.

They ran quickly towards the stable.

"Hey, slow down!" called Camilla after Lynn. "You're running like there's a ghost after you!" Camilla laughed out loud at the memory of Lynn fleeing down the stairs.

Lynn stopped at the stable door and turned to face Camilla. "All you do is make fun of me," she accused, since Camilla had been teasing her all morning. "You have no idea how scared I was last night when I saw that you weren't behind me. I thought maybe you'd been kidnapped or beaten up or something. But no, you just had to sit there and put all the books back like nothing had happened."

"You have too vivid an imagination," giggled Camilla. "You should have seen yourself. First Mephisto discovers a spider or a mouse or something and panics, and the next thing you know you run screaming down the stairs like the devil himself is chasing you. It was hysterical."

"But why didn't you come with me? What if it had been something dangerous?"

"Like what? A ghost?" Camilla shook her head. "I don't believe in ghosts. And besides, I've never heard anything about the attic being haunted. If you're really afraid of ghosts you'd better be careful in the stable."

Camilla raised her arms and flapped them up and down. "Boooo… booooo… I'm coming to get yooooo!" she wailed.

"Cut it out!" Lynn burst out and stormed into the stable, enraged. Here she was, the older of the two, but the more afraid. She would probably get teased about this for the rest of her life, she thought.

But as soon as she entered the stable and smelled the comforting scent of hay and horses, she completely forgot how angry she was with Camilla. Falcon whinnied, happy to have some company. It seemed like he was saying, "Finally, someone's here. I've been waiting forever."

"You don't have anything to complain about," said Lynn, laughing as she entered his stall. She scratched his forehead and pulled on his thick mane. "You got your breakfast long before I did." Falcon snorted and shook his head as if he disagreed.

Lynn led him out of the stall and tied him up. Let's get the most unpleasant chore over with, she thought. She grabbed the manure fork from the wheelbarrow and removed the manure and the wet straw. Then she got out the grooming kit and started to brush Falcon.

"Unbelievable how he can get so dusty again in just one night," she said to Camilla.

"The dust really shows on that color. Why do think I

31

picked a gray horse?" Camilla turned and laughed so that Lynn could see she was kidding. Dust was the last thing on her mind when she had chosen Silvana.

While they were grooming the horses, the subject turned to Elvira's diary. Although they'd flipped through it before going to sleep, they'd been too tired to decipher the ornate handwriting.

"I have the diary with me," said Camilla. "We can have another look at it after we go for a ride."

She put the diary on the feed box. "We'd better hurry!" she urged. "It looks nice out now, but Dad said it may rain later."

Lynn was trembling with excitement as she put Falcon's bridle on him. At last she would know what it felt like to ride a dream horse. Falcon stood still until Lynn tried to put on the girth, then he puffed his belly out.

"No way, my friend!" Lynn laughed. "I'm not falling for that one. I don't really feel like hanging upside down underneath your belly. Got that?"

She led him outside and pulled the girth a notch tighter to make sure the saddle didn't slip while she tried to mount.

It was a beautiful ride. The sun peered out from behind the clouds once in a while, and the landscape seemed made for horseback riding. It was clear that Falcon hadn't been ridden much lately. He tried to take Lynn by surprise a few times so he could take command, but she managed to discipline him every time. Eventually he gave in and accepted that she was the boss.

As soon as they reached the stable again it started to rain. "If that wasn't perfect timing!" exclaimed Camilla.

As she turned the corner, she nearly ran into Eva and Daniel Arnesen, who were standing in front of the stable door.

"Hi!" Camilla greeted them. "Were you waiting for us?"

Eva seemed confused for a second. Then she nodded and said, "We just went for a walk. I thought I heard you talking in the stable just now, so we were about to go in and say hello. That's why I was so surprised to see you coming from around the corner. Your horses are beautiful, by the way!" She carefully reached out her hand to stroke Silvana, but when the horse opened her mouth, she drew it back quickly.

"I have absolutely no experience with horses," she laughed apologetically. "We'd better get inside – it's raining harder."

Lynn and Camilla watched the couple as they hurried towards the house.

∞∞◇◇∞∞

"That's funny. I'm sure I put Elvira's diary on the feed box."

Camilla's eyes searched the stable. Silvana and Falcon were calmly munching hay.

"I know, I saw you put it there. Isn't it there now?" Lynn got up from the blanket she'd laid over a thick layer of straw in the corner of Falcon's stall.

Camilla shook her head. "I don't get it... oh, here it is! But how did it get behind the wheelbarrow?"

"Do you think someone's been in the stable? Why would they move the diary?"

"I don't know. But didn't Eva say she'd heard voices in here when she and Daniel returned from their walk?"

Lynn nodded, remembering it too. "Couldn't it have been Uncle Thomas and Aunt Anne?"

"No way. My mother would have jumped on that diary like a vulture and taken it to the house like some sort of trophy. And she wouldn't have let us see it again until she'd read it through at least five times. I didn't tell you to keep it a secret for nothing."

The girls talked a while longer, but came no closer to explaining how the diary had ended up behind the wheelbarrow.

"Maybe the ghost put it there," said Camilla, to Lynn's annoyance. "Don't start!" she warned her. Lynn couldn't stop thinking about ghosts, but wasn't about to admit it, especially to Camilla.

∞◦◦◦∞

The girls went into Falcon's stall and sat on the blanket. Lynn opened the diary and let her eyes take in the ornate handwriting. How could anybody manage to write such perfectly even letters, she wondered. But even though it was pretty, it wasn't easy to decipher.

"I think we can skip the first few pages," Camilla suggested. "I'm more interested in what Elvira wrote after she met Andrew."

Lynn leafed through to early February of the year of the tragedy. She wrinkled her brow and concentrated on what was there.

"Hey! Here's something about Andrew," she said suddenly. "Listen to this!"

Richmond, February 2nd, 1890

Each day I sit before the window, precisely at the time when my beloved Andrew is done with my father's accounts. Just the sight of his tall, slender figure and his thick, curly hair makes my heart beat faster. Tonight we shall meet again at our secret place in the woods. I have an overpowering fear that my father may know of our secret. I dare not think what he might do! Andrew has asked me to marry him, but how can I tell my father this? He would never in his life accept a man without a fortune as my husband. We must find a solution. The thought of a life without Andrew is unimaginable for me.

∞∞∞∞

"When you know how it ends, it's even harder to read this." Lynn looked up from the diary and gave a start. From where she was sitting she could see the steps up to the hayloft. She thought she'd seen something moving near the steps, but as hard as she tried, she couldn't make out anything unusual.

She held her breath for a moment, but everything was quiet. The only sound was the steady chewing of the horses.

Reading on, the girls realized how terribly afraid of her father Elvira had been. Yet she must have had a strong character, otherwise she would have given in and said "I do" to the bridegroom her father had picked for her.

"I'm glad I'm living now and not back then," admitted Lynn, shaking her head. "Imagine if my father came home and said that I had to marry John! He's the most horrible boy in my class. I feel sick to my stomach just thinking about it. I'd rather walk on hot coals."

"We'd better get back to the house," said Camilla, glancing at her watch, "or else we'll miss dinner."

After dinner Lynn and Camilla helped clear the table and put the dirty glasses and dishes in the dishwasher. Anne brought cups and a full thermos of coffee to the library.

"There's a hockey game on TV in half an hour," said Thomas, who wasn't at all interested in sports himself. "Arnold Stevens and Oliver Dale really want to watch it. They're both rooting for their home teams, so I hope they don't get into a fight."

"Or blast Mrs. Andersen if she shows up and starts to blather," added Camilla.

"That might be the most likely thing. I'll just go and make sure the TV's in order, otherwise they'll be picking on me too," said Thomas and left the room.

"Come on, let's go to my room and read some more of the diary," Camilla suggested. "I don't feel like sitting down here and watching Stevens and Dale yell at each other for an hour like a couple of roaring dinosaurs. It's bad enough listening to them argue during dinner."

When they reached the bedroom, the diary wasn't there. "Didn't you bring it with you from the stable?" asked Lynn.

"Me? I thought you had it. You were the one reading it!"

Lynn tried to remember. She'd had the diary in her hands when she wanted to put on her jacket, which was on a hook on the inside of the door. So she'd...

"Oh no! I put it down on the floor when I went to put on my jacket," she apologized to Camilla, who had settled comfortably on the bedspread with Mephisto in her arms.

"I'll go and get it. Are you coming with me?"

"Can't you go alone? You're the one who left it there. Or don't you dare?" Camilla mocked.

Lynn looked at the window. Although it was relatively early in the evening, the heavy gray clouds made it very dark. Lynn didn't really feel like going out to the stable by herself, but she would never admit it to Camilla. She straightened her back in answer to her cousin's inquiring look.

"Of course I'm not afraid to go out there! What could be dangerous about going to the stable?"

Hurriedly, Lynn put on her jacket and sneakers and marched downstairs. As she opened the front door, she noticed that Mephisto had followed her. He slipped outside along with her and trotted behind her as she entered the stable.

"You're a lot nicer than your owner sometimes, do you know that?" Lynn bent down and stroked the cat's fur. He purred with pleasure and rubbed against her ankles.

Although the stable was dark, Lynn left the lights off so as not to disturb the horses. After all, she was only going to grab the diary and leave. She heard the soft breathing of the horses, but otherwise the place was silent. Lynn squatted down, her hands searching the floor for the spot where she'd left the diary. All she could feel was straw. Had she made a mistake? No, she thought, this is right where I put it. How strange it's not here.

Just as Lynn was about to stand up, she saw a strange, cold blue light out of the corner of her eyes. For a moment it looked like the luminous vague outline of a horse. She froze, cold shivers running down her spine. What was this?

Lynn wasn't sure if she really wanted to know the answer. But her head slowly turned towards the source of the light, as if it had a will of its own. Her heart was beating wildly, and she was totally numb with fear. Then, suddenly, she heard a faint neighing sound. It was hollow and unreal, as if it came from far away.

Gathering all her strength, Lynn stood up and stared at the corner where the blue light had come from. But it was gone, and so was the neighing sound. Had she imagined it? She could not be sure.

But she knew that Mephisto's odd behavior was no imagination. She looked at the cat. He was standing next to the stable door, frozen. His tail was pointing straight up and he was hissing angrily at the empty, dark corner to the right of the door.

Chapter 4
A scream in the night

Lynn lay awake for a long time after she went to bed, thinking of the evening's events. Her cousin could say what she wanted, but something creepy was going on.

Camilla had been startled when Lynn stormed into her room, out of breath. Once she had calmed down enough to speak, she told Camilla about her ghostly experience in the stable.

But Camilla was skeptical. "I'm sure there's a logical explanation," she said. "Couldn't it have been a ray of moonlight or something?"

Except that the sky had been completely clouded over. Besides, the moon didn't look like a horse, and why would Mephisto be hissing at the moon? Aunt Anne had said herself that there were rumors of a ghost in the stable, even if she didn't believe in them herself. And that far-off neighing – how could Camilla explain that? Camilla could only shrug her shoulders. "Fear of the dark and a very vivid imagination," was all she could think of.

Lynn lay in the dark, staring into space. She was afraid and angry at the same time. Why wouldn't Camilla believe her? She'd brushed off the fact that the diary was missing by assuming that Lynn hadn't looked around thoroughly enough. Camilla was sure she'd find it the next morning.

Lynn felt small and stupid. Clearly, her cousin thought she was hysterical and skittish and had run away for no real reason at all. Lynn knew, however, that the explanation wasn't so simple…

∞∞∞∞

What was that? Lynn sat bolt upright in bed and looked at the digital alarm clock on the nightstand. It said 2:16; still the middle of the night. She must have fallen asleep while thinking everything over. But what had woken her up now? She listened, not moving a muscle. Nothing. Had she been dreaming? It was almost eerily quiet in the house. If she tried, she could hear Camilla breathing softly in the bed next to hers. Mephisto, who was lying at the foot of Camilla's bed, stretched out and made a soft scratching noise on the covers. Then it was silent again.

40

No, not completely. There was a creaking in the hallway, as if somebody were walking there. But who could it be? All the guest bedrooms were on the second floor. Anne and Thomas's bedroom was on the ground floor, so they could get to the entry hall quickly if they needed to. Only Lynn and Camilla were sleeping on the third floor. The other rooms still had to be fixed up and were unoccupied now. The only other thing was… the stairway to the attic! That was just where the sound was coming from. Someone was coming down the stairs.

Lynn hardly dared to breathe. Should she wake Camilla? No, Camilla would only make fun of her and come up with some logical explanation.

The footsteps were drawing closer. Shaking, Lynn pulled the covers up to her chin. What if whoever was outside was planning something awful? What if… The footsteps passed the door and went down the stairs to the second floor. Lynn took a deep breath. She was angry with herself for being so afraid. Instead of just lying there like a lump, she should have thrown the door open to see who was sneaking around. But maybe it wasn't too late! If she hurried, with a bit of luck she could still catch a glimpse of their indoor prowler.

She sprang out of bed, tiptoed to the door and opened it, careful to not make a noise. Then she hurried to the stairway. Holding onto the railing, she crouched down and looked through the posts. A lamp on the landing threw a weak yellow light onto the floor, but no farther down. The stairway to the ground floor was in complete darkness. Lynn thought she saw something moving downstairs, but she couldn't be sure. Maybe her imagination was playing tricks on her after all.

She stayed there for a while listening. A soft sound reached her, but from where she was she couldn't place it. There was no way she was going down into that threatening dark stairwell to see if there was really somebody there.

Lynn felt cold after a while and decided to go back to bed. In the morning she could tell Aunt Anne and Uncle Thomas everything. Or could she? Maybe they would think she was letting her imagination get the best of her, too.

She was just about to get to her feet when she sensed there was something behind her. She couldn't hear anything, but she could feel it with her whole body. The fine hairs at the nape of her neck were standing on end. Overwhelmed with fear, there was only one thing she wanted to do: run away! But her legs refused to cooperate. She was frozen to the spot. She only moved when she felt something soft brush against her neck. She jumped up and ran down the stairs as fast as her legs would carry her, letting out a piercing scream that echoed off the walls.

∞∞∞∞

"I've never felt so stupid in my life!" Lynn stared somberly into the glass of milk in front of her on the table.

It was morning, and Anne, Camilla and Lynn were having breakfast. None of the guests had showed up yet.

"They're probably sleeping in after their big scare," said Camilla grinning. "They don't get a drama like that every night – 'A Scream in the Dark' starring the famous Lynn Roberts."

Lynn gave her a dirty look. "Please don't make fun of me, OK? I already feel like such an idiot. Can you imagine how it feels to wake up the whole house because you thought you were being attacked by a ghost or something even worse, and then it turns out to be the cat?"

Anne grinned, shaking her head. "I can imagine how afraid you were," she said sympathetically. "If I'd been sitting on the stairs and a cat had jumped on my neck from nowhere, I would have screamed too, I'm sure."

"Me too." Camilla seemed to be sorry she'd made fun of Lynn. "You should have heard me scream just after we'd moved in to this place, and I found a huge, hairy spider in my bed. If we'd had guests then, they would have all jumped out of the windows from fright."

Lynn had to laugh. Thinking back on the incident, it was pretty funny. She recalled how everyone had yanked their doors open and to see who'd been murdered. Most of them hadn't been too disturbed to see her, but Oliver Dale looked like the sourest lemon in the world.

"Daniel Arnesen must be a heavy sleeper," said Anne, stifling a yawn. "He was the only one who slept through the noise. Only Eva peeked out to see what the matter was."

"And Mr. Stevens didn't want to be seen in his pajamas," laughed Camilla. "He showed up behind the others in a winter coat and slippers. He looked weird!"

The three of them laughed. Just then Thomas came in and said good morning. He looked a bit confused.

"You were right when you said you thought you'd heard something down here," he said to Lynn while he scratched his head. "Someone was here in the entry hall and took that big painting down from the wall. The one that Anne painted."

"You mean they stole it?" Anne seemed almost flattered by the thought that someone would take one of her artworks.

Thomas shook his head. "No, it's still there. But somebody put it on the ground. It's set so neatly against the wall that it can't have fallen by itself. Maybe the person who took it down wanted to steal it, and Lynn foiled his plans with the most blood-curdling scream of the century."

"But Thomas, darling," said Anne hesitantly, "why would anybody steal a completely worthless painting? I mean, the frame is really nice and I like the painting, but it's definitely not worth any money..."

While they discussed these strange goings-on, the guests came down to breakfast one by one. So as not to hear any more commentary about the "nocturnal disturbance", as Oliver had put it, the girls thanked Anne for breakfast and left to visit the horses.

Entering the stable, the first thing Lynn saw was Elvira's diary. It was lying neatly on the ground, precisely where she'd put it the day before.

Chapter 5
A face at the window

Richmond, March 6th, 1890

Something terrible has happened today. My father came home with the announcement that he had found me a suitable husband. I nearly fainted away from shock. Father was so proud of himself and the contract he has made, I felt I would be ill. But when I heard the name of my future husband I felt all the worse – it is that horrible Brian Cookham who lives next to us. He is an uncivilized, arrogant, unbearable man. I would rather die than become his wife! I was so unthinking as to say that to my father's face, and he flew into a rage and roared that I would do as he said or he would make life unbearable for me. I went to the stable and sought the comfort of my beloved horse Alivia, whose soft mane has often received my tears. When she turns her gentle brown eyes to me, I almost feel as if she understands me. But of course that is impossible. I know full well that a simple beast cannot understand what I am going through. Oh, my love! What shall I do? I must speak with Andrew as soon as possible...

∞∞∞∞

Camilla looked up from the diary and pushed Silvana, who was trying to gnaw at her hair, to the side. "Cut it out," she scolded the horse, "there's nothing tasty about my hair! When will you get it?"

"Maybe you shouldn't have used the apple shampoo this morning," Lynn teased her. "Silvana must think you're a walking fruit tree."

"Walking? I'm sitting, aren't I?" Camilla stretched out a hand and patted Silvana, who gave a contented sniff.

The girls had taken a short ride, and now they were sitting in Silvana's stall, reading the diary, which had so mysteriously reappeared.

Camilla was firmly convinced that the diary had been there all along, and the only reason Lynn hadn't seen it the evening before was that she was so nervous and skittish she hadn't really looked for it properly.

However, Lynn was a hundred percent sure that the book hadn't been there. "Look here!" she said to Camilla. "There are a couple of straws under the book, but the floor is completely clean otherwise. I clearly remember that I felt those straws under my fingers when I was looking for the book right in this spot. It wasn't there, I swear it."

"OK, I believe you." Camilla looked pensively around her. "But who could have taken it? And why?"

Lynn couldn't answer that. It was probably somebody who didn't want to be found out. That's why he or she had put the diary back in the same exact spot.

"You don't think Aunt Anne…"

"Of course not, said Camilla firmly. "Then we'd never have seen that book again, and she would have yelled at us for keeping it a secret from her. She's more interested in the Butler family history than Dad is."

Lynn thought about the blue light she'd seen the night before. Could it be… no. That was crazy! There really weren't any book-snatching ghosts around here. There had to be another explanation for these mysterious events.

∞∞∞∞

Camilla began reading aloud again. Elvira was writing about her terror of marrying a man she so clearly couldn't stand. She wouldn't have him for any amount of money.

While Camilla was reading, Lynn stood up and looked into Falcon's stall. He was contentedly chewing on a biscuit she'd put in his feed bucket. She'd had so much trouble getting him dry after riding in the pouring rain. What a shame it was such terrible weather! It wouldn't have mattered so much if Falcon had been her own horse. Then she would have had time to wait for better riding weather. But now her time was limited to a few days of vacation. While she gazed at Falcon's golden back and his lush cream-colored mane, she fell into daydreaming about the two of them out together. She heard Camilla's voice fade away as she sat on Falcon's back and they galloped over the green hills. It felt like flying. The sun was shining and the wind was in her hair...

"Earth to Lynn, Earth to Lynn, can you read me?" Camilla's irritated voice brought her back to reality.

Lynn winced. She hadn't heard a word of what Camilla had been reading for the last five minutes. "Sorry," she apologized. "I was kind of daydreaming."

Camilla smiled. "That's OK. But listen, you've got to hear this — it's getting exciting!"

Lynn sank back down into the straw next to Camilla.

∞∞∞∞

Richmond, March 10th, 1890

Why is Father suddenly in such a terrible hurry? He wants to announce my engagement to that dreadful Brian this Saturday! Has he become suspicious? Does he know I love another? No, that cannot be. Andrew and I have been so careful. When I was in the stable with Alivia today, I had to cry again. She emanates such comfort, that big, loyal beast, as she stands so calmly and endures my outbursts of emotion. After being in the stable I felt more at peace, but now my anxiety has returned. Thank God I am seeing Andrew again tonight. These last few days I have not dared to even look out the window at him, for fear it will anger my father. I must be especially careful when I slip out of the house. I think my father is looking at me strangely.

∞∞∞∞

"If only they'd eloped that night, this whole tragedy wouldn't have happened." Camilla shook her head.

"But they couldn't have known." Lynn turned her head and looked out of the window. It had gotten very dark while Camilla was reading. Blue-black clouds were gathering and shutting out the daylight. "Do you think we'll have a thunderstorm?"

"We might. But you know what I…" Camilla broke in mid-sentence as the stable door opened.

Quickly she hid the diary behind her back, in case it was her mother. The person who stood in the doorway, though, was someone she hadn't expected at all.

Oliver Dale! What on earth was he doing here? He took a few unsure steps.

"Hi!" Camilla greeted him.

Dale looked startled and peered towards the stall where the girls were sitting. Apparently he hadn't expected to meet anyone here.

"Oh! Ah, hello there!" he answered, looking totally taken aback. "I didn't mean to disturb you. I only wanted to…"

He stopped, then continued, "I'm very interested in the construction of old barns and stables, you see, and I

thought I'd just come in and take a look around…"
Again, he stopped, looking very uncomfortable.

Lynn couldn't understand why anyone would feel guilty about something like that. There was nothing wrong with looking inside a stable.

"Please, come on in – you're welcome to look around," Camilla invited him. Oliver mumbled something incomprehensible and turned his back to the girls. He took a quick walk around the inside of the stable, examining the roof and the walls. Then out of the blue he said, "Actually I was still hoping to take a walk before dinner. I'd better get going before it starts to storm."

Then he turned quickly and left. The girls stared at the door in surprise.

"What a strange guy!" said Camilla, shaking her head. "First he wants to see the stable. Then he races around it way too fast to get a close look at anything, then he's gone."

Lynn agreed. Dale had really been behaving strangely. "Do you think he was embarrassed?"

Camilla snorted. "Him? I don't exactly think so when he's constantly criticizing everybody at the dinner table. He's a real… oh, you know what I mean, a…"

"Know-it-all?"

"That's it!"

Lynn laughed for a second. "Do you think he came searching for the diary? That he was the one who took it yesterday?"

Camilla sounded completely convinced. "Yeah, he could be!" Then she frowned and said, "No, actually, he couldn't. If he had taken it yesterday, I'm sure he would want to read the whole thing through before bringing it back. He couldn't assume that it would just stay here in the stable."

Lynn saw that Camilla was right. "I guess he's just a little strange," she concluded with a shrug.

∞∞∞∞

When the girls came into the entry hall half an hour later, they walked straight into the middle of a loud argument. Mrs. Andersen was standing by the coffee table, talking to Anne. She looked very upset and agitated and was waving her hands wildly in the air.

"A very important letter has arrived for me, and I know it. And now you claim that there's no letter at all!" Her voice was almost cracking.

The racket awakened Mephisto, who had been peacefully sleeping on an easy chair near the coffee table. He stood up and glared at the loudmouth who'd disturbed his slumber, switching his tail back and forth and looking like he was about to attack. Camilla ran to him and stopped him from doing any serious damage.

Anne calmly told Mrs. Andersen that she was sorry, but that only made things worse. Mrs. Andersen was getting more agitated by the moment. Who knows where it might have led, if Eva hadn't come down the stairs at just that point. In her hand was an envelope.

"I'm so sorry," she said. "I just opened this letter by mistake. I only saw it was for E. Andersen and not for E. Arnesen after I'd opened the envelope."

She offered the envelope to Ellen, who snatched it from her hand. "Did you read the letter?" she asked venomously.

51

"N-no," Eva stammered, a little flustered. "I'd just opened the envelope when I realized the name was wrong. Then I came downstairs right away. What do you think? Of course I don't read other people's mail." Eva looked very angry.

"I should hope not, young lady!" Mrs. Andersen was really on a roll now. "You should always check the name and address on a letter. It's unforgivable to open someone else's mail."

Eva was just about to say something, when Anne interrupted.

"I'm really very sorry," she apologized. "It's all my fault. I gave Eva the letter by mistake. You should be annoyed with me instead of her. Oh, how embarrassing."

Mrs. Andersen looked around and saw that everyone was staring at her with surprise and disbelief, as if to say, "What a lot of fuss for a little misunderstanding!"

Ellen seemed to realize what they were thinking. With an uncomfortable laugh she said, "Oh, never mind! I should apologize myself. I didn't mean to fly off the handle like that. It's my nerves. I've haven't been feeling well all day. I think I ought to lie down for a little while before dinner." Dramatically she put her hand to her forehead, and without looking at anyone, she went upstairs.

Anne shook her head and gave Eva an apologetic little smile. Then she went to the kitchen to see if Thomas needed help with the cooking.

There certainly are some strange people staying at the hotel, Lynn thought.

"The only thing missing would have been if Mephisto had gotten his claws into her," she said to Camilla, with a giggle. "You know, for a second I was sorry I held him back. But it would be bad advertising for the hotel if word got around that we let vicious animals attack the guests."

During dinner, it seemed as though Ellen had resolved to be extremely polite and friendly, especially to Eva. Her exaggerated warmth got on everyone's nerves. Stevens and Dale, involved in a heated political debate, completely ignored her. A red-faced Oliver was waving his fork around as if that would make his point stronger. For a moment it looked like he was going to stab Arnold with his fork, just for daring to have a different opinion. Fortunately he thought better of it. Dinner ended without any bloodshed.

Afterwards both of them disappeared into the library to continue their discussion away from the others.

"What a couple of hotheads," said Lynn to Camilla, rolling her eyes. The girls helped Anne clear the table. Meanwhile, Thomas brought coffee, cups, and pastries to the library, but nobody really wanted to sit in there since the heated argument was still going on.

"The way those two are behaving, you can understand how wars break out," said Thomas with a shake of his head as he came back to the kitchen.

Lynn and Camilla went upstairs.

"I see Aunt Anne's painting is back in its place," said Lynn as she stroked Mephisto's thick, shiny fur. He was lying curled in a ball on Camilla's bed and now looked incapable of hurting a fly. Lynn scratched him under the chin. He rolled onto his back in the hope of getting a tummy rub. Lynn took the hint and Mephisto started to purr with pleasure.

"I don't understand why anybody would steal art done

by an amateur painter," said Camilla as she ran her fingers through her long blond hair.

"Maybe he took it from the wall thinking there was a safe behind it," said Camilla. "Safes are always behind paintings in the movies." She thought for a minute and continued. "But then he wouldn't have had to take the painting down. He would only have to lift it a little to peek behind it." Camilla threw Lynn a mischievous look. "Maybe your ghost was out exploring."

Lynn stuck out her tongue. "Could you just stop it? Obviously it wasn't a ghost that took the picture off the wall. It was a real flesh-and-blood person. And there are only a few suspects. I mean it has to be one of the guests, doesn't it?"

They mulled it over for a long time, but couldn't get any further. Lynn decided that Stevens was the prime suspect. Camilla thought it was Dale. "He's always sneaking around everywhere and he acts so weird," she said. "And there's nothing to say it had to be a man. If we're talking weird behavior, then Chatty Kathy is another suspect."

Lynn grinned. "Wow, she was really in winning form today! The way she went on you'd think whatever was in that envelope was classified 'Top Secret'."

"We might as well include Eva and Daniel. Then we've got everybody," laughed Camilla.

Lynn wanted to answer, but suddenly she had a thought. It was something about… something like… no. She'd lost it. She shrugged her shoulders. If it was important, it would occur to her again.

"Enough about our strange guests," suggested Camilla. "Let's go say good night to the horses!"

54

Mephisto lifted his head as the girls left. It was clear he wasn't planning to go anywhere this evening.

∞∞∞∞

"Lynn, look!" Camilla pointed at the sky. "You can see the moon. It looks like it's clearing up. And I was sure it was going to rain and storm."

"Maybe we can take a nice long ride tomorrow," Lynn suggested. "That would be great after all the bad weather we've had."

It was quiet in the stable. Camilla had only turned on the light near the door. The rest of the stable was in semi-darkness. Since both of them were there together, Lynn wasn't scared.

She stood for a long time in Falcon's stall, stroking him. He was sleepy and contented, and Lynn could tell that he was relaxed. For a moment she thought of the spooky blue light she'd seen last night, but then she shook off the unsettling memory. She wanted to enjoy this. She was just scratching the top of Falcon's mane when a piercing scream made her jump. Startled, Falcon began to whinny.

Lynn turned around and saw Camilla frozen with fear. The biscuit she had been about to feed Silvana fell from her hand.

"A monster!" she whispered, her trembling hand pointing to the window. "He was out there staring at me. His face — it was all deformed. It was horrible!"

Lynn looked to where Camilla had pointed, but there was only the tree out in the yard silhouetted against the pale moonlight. Lynn felt an icy shiver go up her spine. Who, or what, was lurking out there in the dark?

55

Chapter 6
Footsteps in the attic

"All right! I admit it wasn't a monster." Camilla turned around and glared at Lynn, who was grinning at her from atop Falcon's back.

The weather had turned out exactly as they'd hoped. The horses were rested and in good spirits, the sun was shining down from a nearly cloudless sky, and there was almost no wind. The day was absolutely perfect. Lynn bent forward and gave Falcon's neck a pat. He snorted and threw his head up, tossing his thick mane in the air.

"Oh, sure! So now you admit it. Last night you were

convinced that there was some evil monster lurking outside the stable." Camilla gave her cousin a withering
look. She'd thought that for one moment last night, and
that was all. She could still see that horrible misshapen
face, pressed up against the stable window.

"But there really was someone outside," she said, annoyed. "Of course it wasn't a monster, but it was something horrible." She was silent for a moment, then said
sheepishly, "I guess it serves me right that you don't believe me. After all, I gave you such a hard time about that
ghost and…"

"I believe you," reassured Lynn. "And I promise I
won't tease you about it any more. But only if you admit
that you're not always as cool as you act."

∞∞∞∞

"Know what I think?" asked Lynn while the two of them
rode abreast. "There was somebody outside, like you said.
But it was just a normal person. When he pressed his face
against the window to peek in, it got all squashed so it
looked deformed. Just like you described it."

Camilla looked relieved. Lynn's explanation sounded
convincing. But her relief was followed by confusion.
"But who would want to scare us like that? And why?"

Lynn thought for a moment then said, "Who said that
they wanted to scare us? Maybe they just wanted to look
and see if the stable was empty before they went in."

"Oliver Dale!" The name practically leaped out of
Camilla's mouth. "I'll bet it was him! He was sneaking
around the stable earlier last night. Remember the look
on his face when he came in and saw us there?"

Lynn nodded. "I think you're right. But why? What could there be in the stable that would interest him?"

"The treasure, of course!" groaned Camilla. "He heard my mother talking about how there's a treasure hidden somewhere on the property."

Suddenly Lynn was just as excited as Camilla. "Yeah, that makes sense. And Aunt Anne said there were still some boxes and chests in the attic *and* the hayloft. I'll bet he was going to go looking through them!"

"Well, he would've been disappointed," said Camilla, grinning, "because we've locked the stable and put the key back upstairs."

"Because you thought the monster might come in and eat up the horses," teased Lynn. She just couldn't help herself.

Camilla looked annoyed at first, but then had to laugh. "You know I couldn't think clearly last night. But if we're right about Mr. Dale, then it's really great that we locked him out."

"He must have been the one that took the diary, too. Maybe he was hoping to find some clue about where the treasure is hidden."

Lynn nodded. "We have to read the rest of the diary as fast as we can once we get home. Maybe there'll be something in it that can help us."

But nothing can explain the eerie blue light that I saw in the stable, Lynn thought. That's one mystery I'd like to see cleared up!

They rode on in silence. Lynn savored riding over the wide, soft forest path on such a strong horse. Falcon was a joy to ride. His gait was completely rhythmic and relaxed. When they reached a big open field a little later, she urged him into a gallop for just a little while. The feel of her face in the wind was wonderful, just as wonderful as the daydream she had had. It was too bad that this dream would be over in just a few days, and she would have to say good-bye to Falcon. She slowed him down to a walk and forced herself to focus on other things.

If it was true that Dale was poking around, looking for the old family fortune, then he must have been the one who took down the painting from the wall. She said this aloud to Camilla, who was having the most awful time slowing Silvana to a walk after their gallop. Silvana was tripping sideways, but gradually Camilla got her under control.

"Sometimes she's really ornery," laughed Camilla. "Sorry, what were you saying about Mr. Dale?"

Lynn repeated her suspicion.

Camilla thought it over. "But didn't you say he was the first to storm out of his room when you screamed?"

Lynn hadn't thought of that. Camilla was right. Oliver Dale couldn't have been downstairs and in his room at the same time.

"But who could have taken the painting down from the wall? Rats! I thought we'd solved the puzzle."

"Maybe the painting has nothing to do with anything," volunteered Camilla.

"No, I don't think it does," said Lynn.

When the girls rode up to the courtyard of the estate, the first person they saw was Oliver Dale. He was just stepping out of a taxi, and he didn't exactly look friendly.

Lynn had been planning to ask him directly if he'd

been looking in the stable window last night, but when she saw his angry face, she changed her mind.

"He looks as if something really unpleasant has happened to him," said Camilla while they were unsaddling their horses.

The horses were tired from the long ride, but no too tired to eat. Lynn had to laugh when she approached Falcon with an armful of hay, and he nearly knocked her over in his hurry to get at it.

"Hey, you pig!" She tried to sound strict. "I'd like some food too, but I'm not knocking people down to get it!"

Falcon snorted and stuck his nose out greedily to get more hay. Lynn stood next to him for a minute stroking him, and then went outside where Camilla was cleaning Silvana's hoofs.

The atmosphere at dinner was quiet and tense. Dale still looked grouchy and said nothing. He was shoveling salmon, rice, and vegetables into his mouth, seeming not to notice what he was eating.

That morning Arnold Stevens had announced that he was going to the museum with a few of his students. Anne tried to ease the tension by asking about his day in town.

"Oh, it was extremely nice!" he told her. "We could have used more time to see everything. The students were all very interested, too. It was delightful to be with such nice, intelligent young people."

"But how could that be?" asked Eva, astonished. "I'm sure I saw you upstairs on the top floor. I'd gone back up to get my camera because I'd left it behind when Daniel and I went out this morning. It must have been between noon and 12:30. You'd just gone up the stairs and turned

61

right into the hallway. I only saw you from behind, but…"

Arnold turned and looked at her with raised eyebrows. "I can assure you it wasn't me," he said dismissively. "I was still in the museum at that time."

Eva looked at him in disbelief. "I was so sure that…" But she never got to finish her sentence, because Ellen Andersen let out a loud scream.

"Oh, no, how awful!" she cried. "I've just spilled sauce all over poor Daniel's sleeve."

She went on fussing for some time, clucking like an agitated hen. Despite Daniel's attempts to calm her down, she kept smothering him with apologies. He was so embarrassed by the whole thing that he could only sit there red-faced. Lynn and Camilla didn't dare look at each other for fear they'd burst out laughing. Thomas ran to the kitchen to get a wet cloth, and got most of the sauce out. Once everyone was calmed down, the conversation turned to the history of the estate, and no one returned to what Eva had wanted to say.

Stevens asked Anne a lot of questions, and Lynn had the feeling that he was trying to draw attention away from the previous subject.

∞∞∞∞

Lynn couldn't discuss this strange occurrence with Camilla until after they'd gone to bed later that night. After dinner, Eva and Daniel had asked if they could accompany the girls to the stable to see how they bedded down the horses for the night. It had been a lot of fun, and Eva had dared to feed Silvana a few carrots.

"She doesn't bite, does she?" Eva had asked in a timid voice.

Camilla had showed her how to feed a horse with her hand outstretched. "You have to keep your fingers out of the way," she'd warned Eva. "A horse won't bite on purpose, but if you get your fingers in the way while he's eating something nice, it could happen by accident. But the way you're doing it now is fine. He can't bite you."

When they came into the house, Eva had said enthusiastically she might even take riding lessons.

"That's progress," said Camilla later that night, as she and Lynn brushed their teeth. "At first she was scared to death of horses and now she wants to ride."

"I can understand that she was scared at first," said Lynn. "She said herself that she wasn't used to being around animals. But now that she's seen how nice Falcon and Silvana are, she's a fan. Horses are irresistible! But I've always said that." She put her toothbrush back and went into the bedroom. "Where did you put the diary?" she called to Camilla.

Incomprehensible sounds floated out through the bathroom door.

"Don't talk with your toothbrush in your mouth! I can't understand a word you're saying!"

"Under my mattress," called Camilla. "With all the weird things going on here, I didn't want to leave it lying around in the open where anybody could see it."

Lynn lifted the mattress up and grabbed the diary. "By the way, did you notice how much trouble Mr. Stevens went to today, just to change the subject?" Lynn asked Camilla once she'd come back into the room. Camilla nodded. "Do you think he lied about being in the museum and was here instead?"

"I don't know." Lynn shrugged her shoulders. "But why would Eva claim she'd seen him if she hadn't? With that tall, skinny build and gray beard, you couldn't confuse him for anybody else."

"She couldn't have recognized him by his beard if she only saw him from the back, though, could she?" asked Camilla.

"She might have when he turned the corner and went down the hall. If it really was him, he's behaving just as suspiciously as Oliver Dale."

"Maybe they're both looking for the treasure, either together or separately." Camilla looked expectantly at Lynn.

"Hmm," Lynn murmured, thinking. "Possibly. Whatever the case we should talk to your parents and ask them what they think about it."

"I don't know," answered Camilla. "I mean, nothing really happened. They'll probably just laugh and say what active imaginations we have. Believe me, I know them!"

"We'd better sleep on it and decide in the morning," Lynn suggested. "But let's read the diary some more and see if we can find another clue."

∞∞∞∞

Richmond, March 14th, 1890

So, it is decided. Andrew and I will flee and start a new life together in a new place, as we have so often talked about. Andrew thinks our future lies to the west, and he has family in California where we can stay. Andrew says that anyone who's willing to work hard is welcome there. I am not afraid to work, so that is not a problem, but California seems so very far away. He says it will take us weeks to get there. Of course, I can only take the bare essentials along, but that does not trouble me. Andrew and I will manage. What I most dread is saying good-bye to my beloved Alivia. It would be impossible for me to take her on this long journey, because they would surely track us down. Andrew has planned everything. Tomorrow we shall meet in our secret place in the woods. I shall take as many clothes and belongings as I can carry.

Andrew will have gone to the stable to fetch Alivia. We will pack her up and ride to Andrew's cousin, James, at whose house we will leave her. Andrew thinks Alivia will be safe there. What will happen to James if Father discovers my horse there? I fear for him. Andrew says I mustn't think about it, but I cannot help it. No one knows better than I how irrational Father can be if he thinks someone has deceived him.

Andrew and I will shelter with some other relatives of his along the way. We are going be married as soon as we have arrived in California. How I yearn for that day!

Yet I am so afraid that my father will thwart our plans. I had the oddest feeling today when he looked at me. I am trembling. But now I only have to bear him for one more day. Then I will be free.

∞∞∞∞

"Lynn, wake up!"

"Hmm?" Lynn turned over and tried to escape the sound that was invading her dreams. She had ridden Falcon to the lake and was swimming now, and didn't feel like returning to reality at all.

But the voice persisted, and now someone was shaking her by the shoulder. She opened her eyes, and they met Camilla's. The lamp on the nightstand threw some light onto the bed, but otherwise the room was dark. Lynn looked at the clock. It was 1:30 in the morning. Why on earth would Camilla wake her up in the middle of the night?

"Is the house on fire?" she asked.

Camilla shook her head. "There's someone in the attic," she said in an excited whisper.

Lynn sat up and listened, but heard nothing.

"You must have been dreaming," she said, and was about to lie back down when she heard a thumping overhead, followed by a scraping sound, as if something were being dragged along the floor.

Lynn stared up at the ceiling. Her heart started pounding in her chest. Who – or what — could be rummaging around up there in the middle of the night?

"Come on!" whispered Camilla impatiently. "Now we can find out who's been prowling around the place."

"Shouldn't we tell your parents first?" Lynn wasn't sure about going upstairs on their own.

"Come on!" Camilla urged. "It's got to be Oliver Dale or Arnold Stevens up there, and I want to know which one it is."

"But what if he gets mad and punches us or something?" Camilla could do what she liked. Lynn had no interest in a confrontation with Dale or Stevens, assuming it was one of them, that is. What if it was something far scarier?

A renewed thumping halted their speculation. "That's it!" said Camilla, throwing her head back. "I'm not allowing people to rummage around in my house in the middle of the night. I'm going up there to unmask that creep, with or without you."

Lynn saw that she didn't have much choice. She couldn't just stay behind like a frightened little mouse and let Camilla go upstairs alone. She grabbed a tennis racket from the corner behind the door. Now armed, she tiptoed out to join Camilla, who was already on her way to the staircase.

Mephisto lay contentedly on Camilla's bed. He looked up for a second, then went back to sleep. Lynn envied him as she hurried after her cousin.

Camilla was waiting at the top of the stairs. "On the count of three we'll barge in and take him by surprise," she whispered.

One, two – three!" The door flew open and the girls stared into total darkness. There wasn't a sound anywhere, and the attic was completely deserted.

Had they been imagining those noises? The girls were utterly confused. Camilla had just reached out to turn on the light when she noticed it was not totally dark in the attic after all. Way in the back where the roof met the wall, a ghostly blue light was moving.

Lynn stood completely still while shivers rippled down her spine. Camilla, motionless beside her, was just as terrified. While the two stood there, staring as if they were hypnotized, the light became brighter and took on the shape of a hand. The hand moved very slowly and ended up hovering over one of the chests along the wall. Then it dissolved into nothingness, leaving the attic just as dark as it had been.

Lynn and Camilla looked at each other, trying to comprehend what they had just seen. Then, agreeing in silent panic, they turned and fled down the stairs.

Chapter 7

Do ghosts really exist?

Early the following morning, Camilla was in the stable trying to find a simple explanation for what they had seen. She was making up the most unlikely things. Finally Lynn lost all patience.

"When will you get it through your skull that this isn't about people looking for a hidden treasure? It's something much more mysterious! Have you forgotten that light in the stable I told you about? It was just like what we saw last night, except that I saw it here, in the shape of a horse instead of a hand. You'll never come up with a natural explanation for it if you try for a hundred years."

Camilla glared at Lynn. Then she turned and entered Silvana's stall. Let her sulk, thought Lynn and went to be with with Falcon for a while. I know what I saw, she thought, and now Camilla's seen it too. After all that's happened, she can't still be saying she doesn't believe in the supernatural.

Lynn was scratching Falcon behind his ears, when Camilla came up to her. Falcon put his head on Lynn's shoulder and was clearly enjoying being treated so lovingly. Only a little while longer, then it's over. Lynn sighed, trying to put the unpleasant thought out of her mind. She wanted to enjoy this time to the fullest and not think about leaving.

Camilla cleared her throat. "You're right," she admitted, poking sheepishly at a few pieces of straw with her foot. "There's no natural explanation for what we saw. I just couldn't admit it. The thought that this place could really be haunted was too scary."

"But ghosts don't have to be dangerous." Lynn tried to sound comforting. "I've never heard of one trying to hurt anybody, have you?"

"No, I guess not." Camilla thought for a minute. "You know, they say that Andrew comes back because he has to make his date with Elvira. Well, that's not actually so scary, it's more romantic and sad."

Lynn nodded and asked, "Do you think maybe the things we saw are sort of leading up to what always happens on March 15th?" Camilla stared at her, not understanding.

"I mean, if it's true that Andrew's ghost comes back

70

on the night of March 15th, maybe there are little signs beforehand. I don't know, but…"

"Yes!" exclaimed Camilla. "Sort of like an echo, but from the wrong direction. I bet you're right, even though it sounds weird. This is some sort of echo from the past – leading up to the 15th.

"What is today's date?" Lynn asked.

"Wait. Today is March 12, no, 13," Camilla answered.

"Then it's only two days before Andrew's ghost appears." Lynn felt goose pimples all over her. The thought of a ghost still unsettled her, whether Andrew was friendly or not.

∞∞∞∞

After breakfast Lynn and Camilla tried to explain their theory to Anne and Thomas, but just as Camilla had predicted, her parents didn't take them seriously. They said there was sure to be a logical explanation for everything. Moreover, the girls shouldn't be so suspicious of the hotel guests, especially with so little evidence!

Lynn raised one last argument. "But it has to be one of the hotel guests, who took the di—"

"Ow! I just got a sliver in my finger!" yelled Camilla while she gave Lynn a kick under the table.

"Let me see!" Anne leaned forward, trying to get a look at her daughter's hand. "No, I'm OK," said Camilla hurriedly. "It'll be fine. I'll just go to the bathroom and take it out. Lynn, why don't you come with me?" Without waiting for an answer, she hurried out of the kitchen and ran upstairs. She was already in her room when Lynn came in.

"What's the matter with you!" she hissed. "You almost told them we have the diary!"

"Sorry," Lynn apologized. "It just came out. Sometimes my mouth is faster than my brain. But you didn't have to kick me so hard!" She bent to rub her shin. "I'm going to have a huge bruise!"

"Serves you right, blabbermouth!" said Camilla with a laugh. She ducked as Lynn threw a pillow at her. It missed, but it hit Mephisto. He jumped to his feet and hissed. With daggers in his eyes he stalked out of the bedroom. The last thing Lynn and Camilla saw was his thick tail held straight up, in offense at this attack on his dignity.

The rest of the day passed without any new super-natural occurrences. Lynn and Camilla took another nice ride, but it clouded over in the afternoon. The next day was supposed to be bad weather. That evening they finally had time to finish reading Elvira's diary. Lynn sat on the bed and read aloud.

∞◇∞

Richmond, April 16th, 1890

I have not been able to write for some time. My cares were too great. I have the feeling that my life is over. What has happened seems so unreal yet so immediate, as if it all took place yesterday instead of a month ago.

I awoke that morning filled with anticipation. By nightfall Andrew and I would take our first steps along a new, shared path through life. In between my daily chores I had secretly gathered the things I would take with me to California. Everything seemed so normal that I began to believe all would go as planned. When Andrew left work to go home that afternoon, I watched him, thinking that soon we would be together forever. I could not have known that it was the last time I would see him.

When Father stormed into the house in a rage and forced me to go to my room, I did not know what had happened. I was unable to move, watching my father as he paced about, ranting like a madman. I cannot remember his precise words, but the import was that I was to be married to Brian Cookham as quickly as possible, so as not to shame Father before the town. My endeavors to make him see reason were in vain. He vowed that Andrew would never show his face here again. Then he locked me in my room and left.

The kitchen maid was my salvation. At least, so I thought. I was able to attract her attention when she was outside in the yard for a minute. In haste I wrote a letter to Andrew telling him we had been discovered. I told him not to go near the stable, and I suggested that we meet the next day at our secret place in the woods. In the meantime I would try to convince my father that I was sorry, and that I would agree to his plans for my marriage. Then, I hoped, he would let me out of my room, and I could find a way to escape and meet Andrew.

But something went terribly wrong. Andrew did not receive my letter. I cannot bear to write the details of the tragedy. My beloved Andrew is dead. My father has also died. But his death is an escape from the punishment that was due to him for his crime. I still cannot believe it all really happened. It is a nightmare from which I cannot wake.

Sam Butler, a distant relative of my father's, is now running the estate. Sam is an odd man. He is married and his wife is expecting their first child, but he does not wish her here. She must stay with her parents until the child is born. Sam seems not to be concerned with how she is managing. The only thing he cares deeply about is his art collection, which he has brought here in many large chests and boxes. The paintings and sculptures I have seen are not to my taste, but admittedly I have no understanding of art.

Sam is a quiet and closed person, which suits my present state perfectly. He has, however, talked at length several times during dinner about all the English art experts with whom he is corresponding overseas. Sam is enormously proud of his British connections. Once he showed me a huge pile of letters, probably all from England. He has also bragged several times about how he has brought a fortune onto the estate. A fortune, he says, that will ensure a comfortable existence for his descendants. I can only assume he means these somber paintings and ugly sculptures. I cannot display any enthusiasm, and hardly listen to him. It is as if I am standing next to myself.

I cannot write any more; perhaps later, when my cares do not weigh so heavily…

∞∞∞∞

Lynn looked up from the diary with tears in her eyes.

"That's all she wrote. The rest of the pages are blank. It's so sad to think they never had a life together," she said.

Camilla nodded. Her eyes were wet, too. "Poor Elvira,"

she said softly, "She deserved a happier ending to her beautiful love story."

That night, the girls slept peacefully and undisturbed, with no idea of what was going on downstairs in the house. They only heard about that when they came down to breakfast the next morning. Anne, looking a little confused, greeted them with the words, "I'll never say you girls have over-active imaginations again. I promise!"

The girls looked at her inquisitively.

"You mean you do believe us now?" Camilla asked cautiously.

Anne rubbed a spot on her head. "Yes. After what happened last night, I have to admit that there's definitely something fishy going on here. You can't imagine what happened to me." She paused for a moment. "I was attacked. In my own house!"

Anne sat down at the kitchen table clutching her coffee mug tightly in both hands.

"Attacked! Mom, are you all right?" Camilla asked. Her eyes were wide with fear. "Where's Dad?" she added, before Anne could answer.

"I'm fine. Dad's serving breakfast in the dining room," answered Anne. "He's taking over for me today. I can't go out and look at the guests right now. I'd only be staring at them, wondering which one of them did it."

"What do you mean?" Camilla was almost bursting with curiosity. "How were you attacked?"

"Well," Anne began, "I woke up at about two o'clock. Not because I heard any noises or anything, but because I was thirsty. I got up to get some water from the bathroom, but then I remembered we still had some iced tea in the fridge. The thought of iced tea was so tempting that I put on my robe and slippers and went out to the hall. That's when I noticed the light was still on in the library. I didn't think anything of it. I just figured Thomas had forgotten to turn it off. You know, he does that sometimes."

Anne took a sip of coffee and continued. "So I went in to turn out the light. But the switch is in such an awkward place that you have to go into the room and around the door to reach it. Why would anybody put a light switch there?" She shook her head. "Anyway, the moment I opened the door and took a step into the room, somebody threw something over my head. Before I knew it, I was knocked down. I heard footsteps but I couldn't recognize them. When I finally got to my feet and pulled my head free, he'd gotten away. I was angry and scared at the same time, but what could I do? I felt totally helpless and I didn't have any idea who it was."

"Are you sure it was a man?" asked Lynn, going to her mother and putting her arm around her.

"I don't know anything for sure any more," said Anne, shaking her head. "The only thing I'm sure of is that there was somebody in the library who didn't want to be recognized. And to top it all off, I got the fright of my life when I left the room to find Thomas. Suddenly I saw a hideous creature with wild hair and a terrified face. I almost fainted. But luckily I recognized the monster or I would've woken the whole house up."

"Who was it, Mom?" asked Camilla, on the edge of her seat.

"A terrifying monster," laughed Thomas, who had just come into the kitchen to get more coffee. He put his arms around Anne and hugged her. "It was her own face she saw in the mirror."

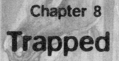

Chapter 8
Trapped

All morning, Anne had to endure her family's supposedly funny remarks. But they were also concerned. The fact remained that she really had been attacked, and by somebody who didn't want to be recognized by her. Anne and Thomas discussed calling the police. Anne thought it would be a waste of time. No one had been injured and nothing had been stolen. "And it would be unpleasant for the guests if the police came and started interrogating everybody," Anne added. "We have to think about that too." Ultimately, Thomas agreed with her.

At noon, when Lynn and Camilla returned from a ride in cold, wet unpleasant weather, Anne appeared in the stable as they were drying the horses.

"Hi!" she greeted them. "Do you want to hear something interesting?"

Silvana gave a loud whinny, as if to say, "Well, out with it! Don't keep us waiting!"

Camilla laughed and patted the horse's neck. "See? Even the horses are in suspense," she said. "What did you find out?"

"Well," Anne began, but Falcon interrupted her. He stuck his muzzle in her hair, which she'd put into a ponytail. He seemed to have found something tasty there and was eager to try it.

Anne pulled her hair to safety.

"Hey, you rascal," she said, raising a finger to him. "What do you think I am? A bale of hay?"

Falcon gave her such a look of pure innocence and utter incomprehension that everyone had to laugh. Lynn took him to his stall and gave him a handful of treats to keep him occupied.

"My guess is that you used that apple shampoo this morning, Aunt Anne," Lynn joked. "Now that he's distracted, what were you trying to tell us?"

"Well, after breakfast I went to look around in the library. I thought that I could find out what our mysterious intruder was looking for last night."

"Did you find anything, Mom?" asked Camilla full of concern.

"Yes and no. I found out whose jacket was thrown over my head. It was Daniel's. He swears that he left it in the library last night, and that could be true. He doesn't have to be the one who attacked me, even if it was his jacket. The intruder might have seen the jacket and thrown it over my head when I came in."

Anne scratched her chin. "I'm not entirely sure what he or she was doing there. But it seems like someone was pawing through the old books in the glass case. There were even a few on the floor this morning. Thomas is certain that they weren't there when we went to bed, because he was the last one to leave the library."

"Maybe the intruder was looking for the diary, hoping it would lead to the treasure," Camilla blurted out. "He doesn't know that we found the..." She stopped abruptly.

Anne looked at her, wide-eyed. "Diary? Are you talking about *the* diary?"

The girls couldn't help but admit that they'd found Elvira's diary. "We were going to show it to you today, since we've finished reading it," said Camilla.

"But why did you keep it a secret? Why didn't you tell me you'd found it?" Anne was visibly irritated. "I've looked through the attic a couple of times for it, and in the library, too. You two had it all this time and didn't say a thing!"

Lynn looked guiltily at the ground, not knowing what to say. Camilla, on the other hand, kept her cool.

"But Mom! If we'd told you, you would've read it ten times before you'd have let us look at it," she said. "I know how you get if you find something new that has to do with Butler family history."

Anne was a little angry at first, but then her face relaxed and she started to laugh. "You're right, too," she admitted with a shake of the head. "I'm afraid I would've done just that. OK, you wanted to read the diary before I got my hands on it. I accept that. But I want you to give it to me as soon as you're done here, got that?"

The girls nodded.

"And now, I want you to tell me everything that has happened to you since this began," Anne demanded. "I'm sure there's a connection with last night's incident."

After the girls had told her about the thumping in the attic, the creepy blue light, and all of the other things that had happened recently, Anne stared thoughtfully into space.

"I have trouble believing this place really is haunted," she admitted hesitantly. "I mean it's a great story, that Andrew returns every year and all that. But I can't really accept it. Frankly, I don't believe in ghosts. I'm sure there's a logical explanation for everything. Trust me, I have no doubt that strange things are happening here. I'm just sure that flesh-and-blood beings are behind them. I would so much like to know what they're looking for!"

"For the Butler family fortune," answered Camilla without blinking. "It can't be anything else. Maybe the person behind all this thinks he'll find a clue to the treasure in the diary."

Anne thought for a moment, shaking her head. "No, I don't think so," she said slowly. "You two told me that the diary disappeared from the stable and then reappeared. That proves that the mysterious nocturnal wanderer has already read it."

"So it can't be the diary he was looking for up in the attic last night," said Lynn. "Then what could it be? Sam

Butler's will, maybe? You said yourself there must be something there about a hidden treasure."

"No," said Anne, "the will is with the family lawyer. But I'm sure I mentioned that when I told the guests the story of Elvira and her tragic fate."

They tossed other ideas around for a while, without getting any further.

"Well, I've got to get back to the house. I've got a lot to do," Anne wound up. "Who knows, maybe I'll get a flash of genius while I'm working. Right now all the guests are under suspicion."

She smiled and began walking towards the door. Just then Mephisto came in. He meowed plaintively and wound himself around Anne's legs.

"Oh, were you looking for me? Afraid you weren't going to get any dinner?" She bent and stroked the cat's silky fur. But instead of the usual purring, Mephisto started and stiffened, his back hair raised. He was staring fixedly at a point to the right of the stable door.

"What on earth…?" Anne stopped, because Mephisto hissed angrily and tore out of the stable, as if a whole pack of dogs were after him.

"He reacted like that once before," Lynn remembered. "As if he saw something creepy in the corner."

"And that's where Lynn saw that blue ghost horse," added Camilla.

Anne knitted her brow. "Now that's really odd. That's the corner where they say Andrew was shot." She was silent for a minute. "But that can't be… No, I don't believe it." She looked at both girls, as if she wanted to say something else, but thought better of it, then walked to the door. She stood there a moment, turned and said,

"Cats have an excellent sense of smell. Maybe there's some odor in the corner that Mephisto's reacting to. That must be it." She seemed relieved, waved to the girls, and disappeared.

"You don't believe that for a minute!" Camilla called after her, but got no answer.

She shrugged her shoulders. "OK, if Mom wants to go on denying the truth, even when it's staring her in the face, I can't stop her!" she mumbled. "I'll bet deep down inside, she knows it's haunted here. She just won't admit it – not even to herself."

Lynn had gone into Falcon's stall and had started to massage his forehead, neck and shoulders. He was clearly enjoying it, because his eyes were half shut and he looked very, very relaxed.

"If you keep that up, he'll fall asleep on his feet," Camilla teased her.

Lynn just smiled but didn't answer. Her thoughts were full of all the mysterious things that had happened. She had a feeling that the answer to the puzzle was right under her nose, but she couldn't see it. She could think about it as much as she wanted, but she couldn't get any further.

By the time the girls were finished the rain had lightened up a little. Still, there were blue-gray clouds hanging like a dark carpet over the landscape, making it a gloomy day.

As Lynn was changing out of her riding clothes, Camilla called from the shower. "Hey, you know what I just thought of?"

"Lunch, I'll bet!" answered Lynn. "I'm starving!"

"OK, OK, first we eat. But then I feel like going up in the attic again and looking at the exact spot where the blue light was. It's better to do it by daylight when it's not so scary."

Lynn felt shivery. After the episode with the luminous hand, she had absolutely no desire to go back up to the attic, daylight or no daylight. But she didn't say that aloud. Camilla already thought she was a coward and she didn't want to make it worse. And a trip to the attic by daylight did seem less scary than one late at night. She shrugged her shoulders and said, "Fine with me."

But it was already evening before the girls got a chance to go to the attic. After lunch, Thomas asked them to help him prepare dinner, which took longer than expected. Then they had to take care of the horses, and before they knew it, it was time for dinner.

"Funny that Mephisto hasn't shown up for his dinner." Camilla pointed to the untouched cat dish on the floor. "It's not like him to skip a meal!"

"Cats do as they please." Anne shrugged. "Don't worry about Mephisto. He will show up when he feels like it."

"Well, we know he's not out hunting mice," giggled Camilla, and the subject of Mephisto was closed.

Dinner was delicious, but being at the table was an ordeal for Anne. She tried not to let her discomfort show, but it didn't work very well. She would forget what she wanted to say while she was in the middle of a sentence, staring at the guests as if she hoped one of them would jump up and say, "I did it."

Of course nobody confessed. They all looked and behaved normally, at least in the beginning. After a while they noticed how strangely Anne was behaving and the mood at the table turned very tense.

Daniel wasn't talking. Instead he was shoveling his

food in as if he was afraid someone would grab his plate and take it away. Oliver and Arnold were making a half-hearted attempt to compare kids' attitudes toward school then and now, and kept looking over at Anne, puzzled.

Only Ellen Andersen was uninhibited. She was telling Eva a long, boring story about her trip to a used book-shop in town. And Eva looked like she wished she were far away. Lynn listened while Chatty Kathy complained about how dusty the store was. "Then those old books got me into such a sneezing fit…" and on it went.

Lynn lost all interest and began talking to Camilla about horses. While Camilla spoke about her plans to go riding with Silvana in the warmer weather, Lynn felt the familiar pangs of jealousy. It would be so nice if she could sit there too, making plans for herself and Falcon. But that was a hopeless fantasy. It wouldn't do her any good to dwell on it.

∞◇◇∞

"We can go to the attic tomorrow, though, can't we?" asked Lynn when they had finished clearing the table. Thomas was making coffee for the guests, and Anne had withdrawn to bury her nose in Elvira's diary. Before dis-appearing, she had told Thomas not to disturb her unless their was a dire emergency.

Camilla answered Lynn, annoyed. "Why should we wait until tomorrow?"

"Because, um…" Lynn couldn't think of an excuse very quickly.

"You're afraid, aren't you?" Camilla asked in a mocking tone.

"Of course not!" As soon as the words were out of her mouth she was sorry she'd said them. But it was too late now. She couldn't take them back.

Minutes later the two were standing by the attic door. Camilla had brought a big flashlight. As they opened the door, they shrank back. Like a cannonball, a large black hissing object hurtled past them. Mephisto! He took no notice of Lynn or Camilla, but shot down the stairs as if the devil were chasing him.

The girls looked after him, shocked. So this was where he'd been. Poor Mephisto! No wonder he hadn't shown up for dinner if he'd been shut in here. But who could have done that? They looked quizzically at each other.

"Turn on the light! I'm not taking one step more if it's dark in there." Lynn said. Camilla looked at her encouragingly and switched on the flashlight. Its bright beam shone on the ground, but there was nothing unusual to see. Camilla took a couple of hesitant steps, and Lynn followed reluctantly. She reached out to turn on the wall switch, pushed it, but nothing happened. The next moment they heard a loud bang.

The attic door had closed.

In a flash Lynn was at the door. She tried to open it, but it wouldn't budge. "Camilla!" she called, frightened. "We're locked in!"

Camilla opened her mouth to say something, but just then the flashlight flickered and died. The girls were in total darkness.

Chapter 9
Elvira's letter

Lynn wasn't sure how long she'd been standing there, paralyzed with fear. She couldn't think clearly, and felt like she'd been hit over the head.

"Lynn? Are you there?" Camilla asked, her voice shaky. "I can't see a thing."

Lynn opened her mouth, but couldn't get a word out.

"Lynn?" Camilla's voice sounded even more anxious.

"I-I'm here," Lynn managed to say. When she felt something touch her arm she nearly screamed. Then she realized it was Camilla's hand. Lynn grabbed it thankfully and drew Camilla to her. The girls held each other and stared, horror-stricken at a corner of the attic. It was no longer dark. A thin, bluish fog was rising from it. It thickened, into a sort of ball and then took the shape of a...

"Look! It's that hand again!" Camilla whispered.

The luminous blue hand hovered in the air for a moment, then slowly floated through the room and stopped above a chest. The hand dropped down, almost onto the lid, where it stayed motionless for a few seconds. Then as quickly as it had appeared, it dissolved into nothing, leaving the girls back in complete darkness. Suddenly the electric light went on, and the flashlight began working again.

Lynn and Camilla heard a sound behind them and wheeled around. It was the attic door. Now it was wide open.

Lynn was just about to run through the door when Camilla said, "You can't go now! Don't you want to know what the hand was trying to show us?"

Hesitantly, Lynn turned around. She glanced behind her, afraid that the door would shut and the nightmare would start all over again.

"This is the second time that hand has appeared up here," said Camilla excitedly. Her fear was gone. "It doesn't want to hurt us. I think it's trying to show us something."

Soon they were kneeling by the chest where they'd seen the hand hovering. The lid creaked when they opened it. Lynn glanced back over her shoulder, not feeling very safe at all. But then her curiosity got the better of her.

The girls pawed through the chest. "Just old account books and letters," said Camilla, disappointed.

Lynn examined a bundle of letters a little more carefully. "These are really old," she said. "And most of them have English stamps. Didn't Elvira say something about how her cousin was so proud of his English pen pals?"

Camilla nodded. She read a few letters, but the contents weren't the least bit interesting and had nothing to do with the estate. Camilla was about to put the bundle back, when she noticed a letter that looked different from the others. She removed it.

"Look at this!" she said to Lynn. "There's no stamp and there's nothing on the envelope." Carefully she opened it and drew out a folded sheet of writing paper.

"It's Elvira's letter to Andrew!" she said excitedly. "The one where she warns him not to come to the stable. Listen to this!"

∞∞∞∞

March 15th, 1890, in haste

My dearest Andrew,
I hope and pray that this letter reaches you in time. The kitchen maid has solemnly promised that she will give it to you. The worst you can imagine has happened. My father knows of our plans to flee. How he has found out, I do not know, but it matters not, for presently my only care is for your safety. Do not, by any means, come to the stable tonight! My father will be waiting for you, and God only knows what may happen.

Come to our secret place tomorrow! I will try to mislead my father into believing I have agreed to his plans. With luck, perhaps I can escape. If I am not successful tomorrow, wait for me the following evening. Somehow I shall manage this. I know it.

Be careful, my darling! We shall see each other soon. This is the only thought that sustains me.

Yours forever,
Elvira

∞∞∞∞

That night Camilla dreamed she was on the estate but it looked completely different. A woman was sitting in a room full of old furniture, feverishly writing a letter. She looked desperate. Just before she was finished, there was a knock at the door. The woman quickly asked a question and seemed to get the answer she expected. With trembling fingers she folded the letter and put it in an envelope. Then she slid the envelope under the door and breathed a sigh of relief.

In her dream, Camilla floated through the wall to the room next to the first. There was a young servant girl in a blue dress that reached to her ankles. On top of it she wore a white apron and on her head was a white starched cap. Just at the point Camilla saw her, she stuck the envelope in her apron pocket. Then she went down the stairs. She walked towards the front door to leave the house, but before she reached it, a stern-looking lady wearing similar clothing stopped her. They must be the cook and the kitchen maid, thought Camilla.

The kitchen maid tried to say something, but she was

pushed through a door that seemed to lead to the kitchen.

Next Camilla was in front of the stable. It was dark both inside and out, and she could hear horses snorting and scraping their hoofs. Then a shadowy figure appeared. Suddenly she heard footsteps and saw a young man hurry towards the stable. He looked around constantly, as if searching for something.

"Don't go in there!" cried Camilla as loudly as she could. But he didn't hear, and walked purposefully towards the stable.

Camilla tried to stop him. She leaped in his path and waved her arms at him, but he walked right through her as if she weren't there, and disappeared into the stable. Immediately there was the sound of a scuffle from in-.side, then a loud boom, followed by panicked neighing and kicking of hoofs. Just before Camilla woke up, she heard a female voice whisper urgently, "You can help this come to an end. You still have a chance. Help us, please!"

Camilla woke with a start and she felt her heart racing. That voice – had it been part of the dream or was it real? She turned on the bedside lamp. Its weak light was comforting. Camilla looked over at Lynn's bed. Elvira's letter was on the night table; Camilla could vaguely see the contours of the envelope. She lay back down and stared at the ceiling, while she went over the details of the dream.

∞∞∞∞

"You know what? We'll tell my mother about the letter tomorrow."

91

"Huhhh…what? Why wait until then?" Lynn wasn't quite awake yet. She was just pulling on her jeans.

"I'll tell you why on the way to the stable. Come on, hurry up! The horses are waiting!"

When they came downstairs, though, something else drew their attention. As they neared the library, they heard noises from behind the door. It was closed, but it was obvious that someone was doing something in there. Who could it be, so early in the morning?

Curious, the girls tiptoed to the door. Camilla glanced at Lynn, turned the knob, and silently opened the door. There was Arnold Stevens, looking at the old books in the glass case. He gave a start when he saw the girls.

"What are you doing here?" asked Camilla evenly.

Arnold smiled, but Lynn thought it was a very sour smile.

"Oh, I just woke up really early this morning," he explained, "and I thought, at last I can look at all those lovely old books in peace. You know, in the evenings, there are always people in here, especially that chatterbox Ellen Andersen. Sorry for saying it, but that's just the truth. You just can't think straight when that silly woman is talking your ears off. So I thought now would be a good time to finally look through the library. I'm very interested in old books, you know."

He looked at his watch. "Oh, my goodness!" he exclaimed. "It's good you came in. Otherwise I would have forgotten the time. I have to give a lecture to 80 students and I still have to prepare. I'd better get going."

With these words, he left the room. The girls watched him go.

"I'll bet he was the one who was sniffing around here the other night and attacked Aunt Anne," said Lynn.

92

"I'll bet you're right," answered Camilla. Come on, let's go find my mom and tell her! But remember, not a word about Elvira's letter!"

∞∞◇∞∞

"How can we prove that Mr. Stevens is the guilty one, and find out what he was looking for?" Lynn glanced up from currying when she heard Camilla's voice. She'd been so lost in thought that she barely realized she was grooming Falcon. She felt guilty and scratched his forehead. He seemed not to have noticed her absent-mindedness and chewed on a few mouthfuls of hay. Lynn, stared sadly at the beautiful horse. His just-brushed coat gleamed like gold and he was so sweet that she wanted to kidnap him and keep him forever.

She sighed. She hadn't been able to ride as much as she'd hoped, either. The weather really hadn't co-operated. Although right now it wasn't so bad…

"There you go, daydreaming again," said Camilla, in a tired voice.

"Sorry!" Lynn apologized. "I was just thinking about other things. What did you say?"

"I was wondering how we can prove Arnold is the guilty one." Camilla looked across Silvana's back at Lynn.

Lynn shrugged. She was more preoccupied with their plan for this evening. Would it work?

"Well, you're not much help," complained Camilla.

"Could we set a trap for him or something?" suggested Lynn.

"What kind of trap?"

To Camilla's great disappointment, Lynn didn't have an answer. Anne hadn't come up with anything either, when they'd told her about their suspicions. Camilla had the feeling her mother wasn't taking this very seriously. Then as she turned her head she bumped it. Grumbling, she brushed Silvana and waited for an idea to come. But it didn't.

The girls saddled up the horses and silently made the last preparations for the ride. When they'd left the stable and the cool breeze was in their faces, Camilla's mood improved.

"Sorry I was so grouchy back there," she apologized. "But it makes me angry that there are things going on right under our noses and we can't figure them out."

Lynn didn't answer. She wanted to concentrate on riding, not ghosts and secrets. She had been looking forward to this vacation so much, to being out on a horse, and as free as the wind.

Lynn put Falcon into a canter and delighted in how willing he was to cooperate.

But her happiness was short-lived. In record time, black clouds gathered overhead and the day turned dark and gray. Once the rain started, they had no choice but to turn around and go back home.

Two soaking wet, sulky riders on two equally soaked horses finally reached the stable. The rain pounding on the ground drowned out the horses' gentle hoofbeats.

The girls dismounted and Camilla slid the stable door open. When they led the horses in, they heard something strange. They stood still and listened. There it was again.

"Someone's up in the hayloft," whispered Camilla, pointing upwards. Lynn, who was already freezing cold, suddenly got even colder. Who could it be? Not Anne or Thomas, that was certain. At this time of day they had too much to do in the hotel.

Camilla put her finger to her lips. As silently as they could, they led the still-saddled horses to their stalls. The rain drummed on the roof so hard that it drowned out most of the sound.

Camilla went up the stairs first, and Lynn followed reluctantly. A new sound from above gave her the shivers. They crept up the steps one by one, ready to retreat at the first sight of anything scary.

Once they were at the top of the stairs Lynn craned her neck to look at the hayloft. To her relief there was nothing to see; the loft looked completely empty. They must have imagined that noise. Then she saw Camilla pointing to the door of the supply shed. "That door is open," she whispered in Lynn's ear. "We always keep it closed."

Curious, the girls went to the door and cautiously peered inside. There was no one to be seen. Hesitantly they stepped inside.

Lynn wheeled around when she heard the sound behind her, but it was too late. The door closed with a loud bang, then they heard a key turning in the lock.

Chapter 10

A murderer returns

"Help! Help! Let us out!" Camilla screamed as loudly as she could and banged her fists on the door.

"You might as well stop! No one can hear us in here." Lynn stepped over to the dusty skylight and looked outside. It was still pouring, and the water running down the window blurred the landscape. The girls had been locked inside for nearly an hour now; an hour filled with panic, doubt, and vain calls for help. The stable was too far from the house for anyone to hear them. And with this weather it wasn't very likely that somebody would be walking past the stable by chance. Even Daniel and Eva, the most outdoorsy of them all, were surely huddled up inside by the fire.

"Brrr, I'm so cold." Lynn was shivering in her soaking wet clothes. "And the poor horses! They're downstairs dripping wet with their saddles and everything still on!"

"Just wait until I get out of here!" said Camilla angrily. "Arnold Stevens isn't going to get away with this."

"But how do you know it was him?" asked Lynn. "We didn't see who was hiding behind the door. It could have been anybody – Oliver, Eva, Daniel, or even Chatty Kathy."

"I just know it was Stevens," said Camilla with complete confidence. "We agreed he was behind all those mysterious events, didn't we? He's not the ghost, but he's behind the rest of it!"

"Yeah," murmured Lynn hesitantly. "But didn't he leave early this morning in a taxi to go to town? Do you think he's back already?"

"I'll bet anything the taxi to town was only an alibi, so he could come back here and snoop around some more. He probably only went a little way in the taxi and then walked back through the forest, so he wouldn't be seen. Wait till we get out of here, then I'll check out his alibi! I'll bet you a new pair of riding boots he didn't have any lecture in town today. What do you think?"

Lynn shook her head. "I don't think…" she began, but she stopped when she heard a voice downstairs in the stable.

"Hello! Is there someone there?"

Lynn never thought in her wildest dreams that she

would be happy to hear Chatty Kathy's voice, but right then it was the most beautiful sound in the world.

"We're up here," they yelled together. "Somebody locked us in."

First they heard a long and unintelligible stream of words followed by rapid footsteps coming up the stairs, then someone rattled the door trying to open it. But of course it wouldn't open.

"It's locked!" cried Camilla, impatient because Mrs. Andersen had missed the point entirely. They'd already said they were locked in. Why would she think she could just walk up and open the door?

"But there's no key here." Ellen Andersen sounded totally confused. "Are you sure it's not in there with you?"

"If we had the key with us, we wouldn't be in here," answered Camilla trying to control what temper she had left.

After a few moments Mrs. Andersen said, "I'm going to the house to get your father, Camilla. Maybe he has a spare key."

The girls heard her thump down the stairs and slam the stable door behind her. They sat heavily on a couple of boxes. In five minutes or so, Thomas was outside the door with the tool chest.

"Don't worry, girls. It'll just take a second," he said comfortingly, and set to work on the lock.

It took another half hour, because the screws were old and rusty, so it was hard to turn them. Eventually, Thomas was able to open the lock and the girls were free.

∞∞∞∞

"I just can't imagine that Mr. Stevens would be behind this." Thomas shook his head in disbelief.

It was an hour later. The girls had unsaddled the horses and dried them off. Then they'd come back to the house and had nice hot showers. Now they were sitting in the kitchen with their hands wrapped around steaming cups of hot chocolate, telling Anne and Thomas what had happened. They'd mentioned their suspicions about Arnold.

"Well, we can find out about that easily," said Anne, grabbing the telephone. "Where did he say he was giving the lecture? At the university, right?"

Anne called directory assistance and got the university phone number. A moment later she was connected to the switchboard.

It seemed like a century before she hung up. Anne sighed. "I got put through to five different people before anybody could tell me if Stevens gave a lecture today."

"And? He didn't, did he?" Camilla looked triumphantly at her mother.

"Yes, he did," said Anne, with a sorrowful little smile. "He not only gave a lecture, but he's still there and is having lunch with some of the students. So, whoever locked you two in there was not Arnold Stevens."

"I just don't get it!" Camilla turned to Lynn and waved her currycomb in the air. "We were so sure that Mr. Stevens was our villain and now he's got a watertight alibi."

Later in the afternoon, the girls were back in the stable. This time they stayed well away from the hayloft, even though the lock had been removed and nothing could happen. While waiting for Thomas to free them from their prison, they'd passed the time by looking through the old chests and cases in the shed. They had found nothing that would interest treasure hunters. Even Thomas had looked around, but he hadn't found a single clue to what someone could be looking for up there.

Lynn pondered over everything while she untangled Falcon's mane. He whinnied softly and blew warm air at her neck. Lynn stroked his velvety nose. Luckily the horses didn't seem to have suffered any ill effects from being left, cold and wet in the stable. What a lucky break it was that Ellen had come and found them, or who knows how long they might have been trapped in that freezing hayloft! Lynn suddenly had an idea and turned to Camilla.

"I wonder what Chatty Kathy was doing in the stable in the first place. Can you explain that?"

Camilla looked at her, astounded. "I didn't even think of that! I was so happy that somebody came to get us out of there. Now that you mention it, it is pretty strange."

"Do you think she could have locked us in?" asked Lynn. "What if she was behind all of this?"

"Chatty Kathy? I can't believe she'd have the brains to be behind anything," responded Camilla.

Lynn secretly admitted Camilla was right. She couldn't imagine this empty-headed woman was capable of systematically combing the estate on a search for a treasure. There must be some other explanation for her turning up in the stable. They would definitely have to ask her that when they got back to the house.

"But if neither Arnold nor Chatty Kathy were looking for the treasure, who could it have been?" Lynn asked her cousin. "If we're still right about it being a hotel

101

guest, the only people left are Oliver, Eva, and Daniel."

"If I had to pick anybody, I'd bet on Oliver Dale," said Lynn. "He was hanging around the stable and acting really strange. But we could be on the wrong track altogether. Maybe it's none of the guests."

"But it has to be. If there were a stranger poking around here day and night, we would have noticed by now."

Camilla pushed her hair back from her face. "In mystery stories the one who did it is always the one you least suspect. Who's that?"

"Your mom," giggled Lynn. "The explanation for everything is that in reality, Aunt Anne is a female 'Dr. Jekyll and Mr. Hyde'. By day she's normal and nice, but by night she changes into a monster that sneaks around and attacks people."

"You're nuts!" Camilla stuck her tongue out at Lynn. "Come on, be serious. Who could it be?"

Lynn shrugged. "It actually could be any of them. We were so wrong about Mr. Stevens, it doesn't make much sense to guess any more.

Lynn agreed. "And if it's Eva and Daniel, they're working together, of course."

"Maybe it is them," Camilla mused while she continued combing Silvana. "You know, it could be. Remember when Mephisto attacked you, and you woke up everybody with your screaming?"

"Stop it! Please," Lynn begged. "That was so embarrassing."

"But one person didn't wake up from all that noise. Remember how strange we thought that was?"

"Daniel!" exclaimed Lynn. "You're right! That's what I couldn't put my finger on before. He didn't wake up.

Maybe he wasn't even in his room. Maybe he'd taken the painting off the wall downstairs and was hiding until he thought the coast was clear!"

"I think we're finally on the right track," said Camilla excitedly. "But if they wanted to steal the painting, why didn't they just take it later on?"

Lynn shook her head. She didn't understand that either. She thought for a moment, then an idea came to her. "I think I've got it!" she cried. "Daniel took the painting down from the wall and studied it. He had to determine that it was as worthless as Aunt Anne said it was. That's why he just left it there."

"Right, and so they had to keep on looking, because they had absolutely no idea what the hidden treasure was." Camilla scratched her head.

"Exactly," confirmed Lynn. "The only thing in Elvira's diary about it is that her cousin told her something about insuring the family's fortune. But she never got to hear what it was."

"And there was nothing about it in the will either," said Camilla. "Otherwise it would have been found long ago."

"If only we knew what kind of treasure it was," sighed Lynn, "then it would be a whole lot easier to trap the treasure hunters." As much as they thought about it, they couldn't find an answer.

"I give up," Camilla confessed, patting Silvana on the neck as she left the stall.

"Me too." Lynn stroked Falcon's mane and joined Camilla. "We can think about it some more tomorrow. Tonight we have more important business."

"Good thing the weather's cleared up," said Camilla

happily as they slipped out of the hotel's back door late that evening. Under their arms they each carried a wool blanket.

"Otherwise the most important part of our plan would have gotten all washed up – literally!" Lynn put a hand in her pocket to make sure the letter was still there. "So what did you think of Chatty Kathy's explanation for being in the stable?"

Of course the girls' adventure in the hayloft had been a subject of discussion at the dinner table that night. Everyone had been shocked (or at least pretended to be) to hear that someone had locked them in.

Anne had discreetly questioned the guests one by one to find out where they had been at the time, but she hadn't found out much. Oliver said he'd gone to a museum. Eva and Daniel said they'd gone to town to do some shopping. "It was a cheap trip," Eva had said. "We hardly bought anything."

Only Arnold had a watertight alibi.

Camilla had asked Ellen why she had gone out to the stable in such awful weather.

"Oh, because of that note, of course," she'd answered, as if she thought everyone knew what she was talking about. Seeing all the questioning faces looking at her, she added, "I was lying on my bed resting, when suddenly I heard a knock at my door. Then a paper was shoved under the door before I could even get up. All that was written on it was: 'Go to the stable'. Of course I was terribly curious, so I changed my clothes and went out there right away."

∞∞∞∞

104

Camilla pressed the blanket more tightly to keep it from slipping out from under her arms. "I don't know," she said uncertainly. "Chatty Kathy's story is so unlikely, it's almost got to be true."

Lynn nodded and almost tripped as Mephisto shot out of the dark and walked right in front of her. He meowed plaintively and looked longingly at the door. Lynn grinned, turned back to the door, and let him into the house. He obviously wasn't very interested in coming along to the stable.

As they walked along the gravel path, the clouds parted and a silvery moon appeared. It made an eerie reflection in the puddles and on the trees, which were still wet from the day's rain. Lynn started feeling very uneasy. What on earth were they doing? What could they do if something went wrong?

Camilla interrupted her train of thought. "Look, there at the edge of the woods! Is that a deer?"

Lynn looked over where Camilla was pointing, but only saw trees.

Camilla carefully slid the stable door open, as if she were afraid that there was someone lurking in the stall. When Lynn went to turn on the light, Camilla hissed, "Are you crazy? We can't turn on the light! It could mess up the entire plan!"

Lynn shuddered. The thought of having to sit and wait in a dark stable until something happened wasn't exactly enticing. But Camilla's idea was worth a try; she had to admit that.

The only source of light other than the pale moon came from the outside bulb over the stable door. Would that be enough? They would find out soon enough.

Lynn quickly pulled the envelope from her pocket and removed the letter. "Got the thumbtacks?" she asked.

"Here!" Camilla gave them to her and Lynn tacked the letter to the outside of the door where the light shone down on it.

Now all they could do was hope that it wouldn't start to rain.

They waited for a long time. Lynn and Camilla had wrapped themselves in the blankets and were sitting in Falcon's open stall where they had a good view of the stable door.

"But what if he… that horrible old man… shows up and sees the letter first?" asked Camilla suddenly.

Lynn looked at her, startled. That hadn't occurred to her at all. She shrugged her shoulders. "Then the whole plan falls through," she said. "But it's too late now. We can't change anything. We can only hope that doesn't happen."

Camilla nodded.

It was silent for a moment.

At last Lynn yawned and said, "Can't we just go back now and get to bed? If everything goes according to our plan, it won't matter if we're here to see it or not."

"Go ahead if you want to," answered Camilla. "I'm staying! I wouldn't miss this for anything. And I don't know what you're scared of now. Nothing can happen to us."

"It could be really dangerous," said Lynn defensively. "How much experience do you have with ghosts?"

Camilla didn't answer. The girls were quiet for a while. Lynn wanted more than anything to return to the house, but something was holding her back. Her curiosity to know what would happen was stronger than her fear. The stable smell and the horses' regular breathing calmed her down, and it was nice and warm under the blanket. Actually, it is pretty cozy sitting here, she thought, and not dangerous at all...

∞∞∞∞

Lynn awoke with a start, sat up, and looked around. She must have fallen asleep. She looked over at Camilla, who had dozed off too. Lynn adjusted her position and shut her eyes to go back to sleep. Then a sound made her jump. What was that? She heard footsteps nearby. Somebody was there! She stopped herself from crying out just in time. She turned to Camilla and saw that she, too, was awake and frightened. Lynn was angry with herself for not going back to the house when she could have. Now it was too late. Her only comfort was the thought that Camilla was just as afraid as she was.

The girls sat motionless, hardly daring to breathe. While they watched, a blue mist rose in the corner next to the stable door. Out of the mist stepped a male figure, and for a moment he was illuminated by moonlight coming through the window. Lynn squinted to see him better, but all she could see were fuzzy outlines and the stable wall showing through his shape. The man was holding something in his hand that glowed dully in the weak moonlight. Was it an old pistol?

Behind Lynn, Falcon began to move restlessly back and forth, as if he sensed that something wasn't right. Silvana seemed to agree with him, and neighed softly as she stamped on the ground.

"Look at that!" whispered Camilla in Lynn's ear.

More blue mist slowly took on the shape of a horse, which was also semi-transparent. Even though the blue cloud was spinning and swirling, they could see that the horse was beautiful and well proportioned. It was big and strong, but very graceful.

Lynn had no doubt that this was Elvira's horse, Alivia. The blurry male figure had pressed himself into the corner of the stable so that he was almost entirely hidden behind the horse. Alivia seemed not to take notice of him. She moved uneasily back and forth and suddenly started to whinny. The sound was strangely muffled, as if it came through a thick wall of fog, but Falcon and Silvana had heard it and reacted by neighing nervously.

Then the girls heard footsteps approaching outside. A moment later the door latch rattled.

Don't come in! Lynn thought desperately. He's here, waiting for you!

Outside, Lynn thought she heard the rustle of paper. She hoped it wasn't her imagination.

The blue light in the corner got brighter and started to pulsate intensely. Lynn had a terrible foreboding. Camilla must have felt the same, because she grabbed Lynn's hand so tightly it seemed she would never let go. The shadowy male figure straightened itself and crept towards the door, pistol hand raised. Lynn felt herself getting queasy. Were they going to witness poor unsuspecting Andrew being murdered as he walked into Alan Butler's trap yet again? Suddenly they heard the footsteps outside running away.

An angry wailing came from the corner next to the stable door and a blue whirlwind rose to the roof. The next moment, all traces of Elvira's father had disappeared. The blue shining horse was still there. It shook its head, tossing its mane. But it, too, began to fade and eventually disappeared. The last thing the girls heard was a muffled, very distant neigh. Then it was just as dark and silent in the stable as before.

Chapter 11
Caught in the act

"Did you see that?" Camilla stood up on trembling legs and turned to face Lynn. "That man and the ghost horse?" Her face was as white as a sheet.

Lynn walked over to Falcon and buried her fingers in his warm, soft mane. She felt like she was dreaming. What they had just experienced was so terrifying it was almost unbelievable. But it must have been real if they had both witnessed it.

"I… saw it too." She couldn't get any more words out. Camilla's plan to hang up the letter on the stable door had seemed logical enough, but she hadn't wholeheart-edly believed that anything would really happen.

Falcon snorted gently and rubbed his head on her shoulder. He was completely relaxed again. Lynn stroked his forehead absent-mindedly while she tried to make sense of what had happened. It was totally unreal. But it had happened. Even the horses had reacted to it. Lynn was cold, and it wasn't just because she didn't have the blanket around her.

As always, Camilla seemed to recover first. "You know what I think?" she asked excitedly. "I think we really were able to make things go differently this time. Just like we planned. Andrew didn't come into the stable, so Elvira's father couldn't do anything to him. Did you see how he whirled up and disappeared?"

Lynn nodded and laid her head against Falcon's neck. "That was so scary," she admitted. "And that horrible scream! Do you think he's gone forever?"

"I hope so!" Camilla's teeth chattered. "I thought he was more disgusting and meaner than the way Elvira described him in her diary."

"Do you think Andrew actually read Elvira's letter?"

Camilla nodded. "Otherwise he would have come into the stable, like he's always done. But maybe we'll find out tomorrow…"

"What do you mean tomorrow?" Lynn looked at her cousin inquisitively.

"Never mind!" answered Camilla quickly. "We'll talk about it later. Now we have to get home. I'm cold and exhausted."

Lynn stroked Falcon's mane and kissed him good night. Camilla was already at the stable door. "Don't forget to take the letter down!" said Lynn to her cousin. "Aunt Anne will never forgive us if we leave it there and anything happens to it."

∞∞⋄∞∞

"It can only have been Andrew. He must have taken it with him," said Lynn as they walked back to the house.

"That's the only possible explanation."

"It's a good thing we hadn't told Mom anything about the letter yet." Camilla jumped over a puddle. "You know the old saying, what you don't know won't hurt you!"

"You could just tell her the ghost took it with him," giggled Lynn. Slowly the tension was leaving her body and she could feel relief and fatigue beginning to replace it.

"Ha, ha. A very likely explanation!" Camilla shook her head. "We've just seen ghosts with our own eyes and we still can't believe it. You can just imagine how my mother would react if we told her."

Everything they had gone through that night was spinning around in Lynn's head. All she wanted was a nice warm bed. Once they got to the house, they opened the back door and went quietly inside.

There was no light in the entry hall. Lynn went over to turn it on, Camilla followed her, and then she bumped into something large, soft, and... alive!

Lynn's scream was just as blood-curdling as when Mephisto had scared her half to death. The response was tremendous and immediate. Doors opened, both downstairs and on the second floor, and a few seconds later the

113

entry hall was bathed in light. Lynn and Camilla stood still and stared into the face of...

"Mr. Stevens! What on earth is the meaning of this?" Thomas, in his pajamas, straightened his tangled hair with his fingers as he looked in confusion, first at Stevens and then at the two girls. "And what are you two doing here in the middle of the night, fully dressed?"

Nobody answered him. Lynn was staring intensely at the box Mr. Stevens was holding. She'd seen it somewhere before.

Camilla was the first to recognize it. "The old letters!" she cried and looked accusingly at Stevens. "They were in a chest in the attic. What are you doing with them?"

Arnold stood stiff as a board and said nothing.

Now everyone came down. They were all there: Oliver Dale, Mrs. Andersen, Eva and Daniel. "I think you owe us an explanation!" Anne strode resolutely over to Arnold and grabbed the box from his hands. "What are you doing in the middle of the night with those letters?"

"I... um..." Arnold seemed to be desperately trying to think of something. "I'm very interested in old attics and documents, as you know. I just wanted to read through these letters in peace and..."

"And you didn't think of asking if it would be all right to borrow them?" There was fire in Anne's eyes and everyone could see she didn't believe a word of what he was saying.

Stevens looked around from one face to another.

"Oh, my goodness, what a scene. I think I'd better go to my room," said Mrs. Andersen, who turned with an apologetic smile and walked to the stairs. It was then that

114

Lynn realized both Ellen and Arnold were fully dressed.

That's funny, she thought. But then, Ellen Andersen tripped on the first stair. When she stood up, something fell out of her jacket pocket. Letters!

She quickly bent down to pick them up, but Camilla was faster and swiped them away in front of her nose.

"What! How dare you…" began Mrs. Andersen, but Camilla interrupted her.

"These are more of the old letters that were in the attic, I'll bet you anything!" she cried, holding them over her head.

"I think you'd better stay down here," Thomas said to Ellen in a sharp voice. "It looks like you and Mr. Stevens have something to tell us."

To Lynn and Camilla's great disappointment, this statement was the last they heard. Anne sent them up to bed and wouldn't take no for an answer.

"I think you two have a little explaining to do, yourselves, don't you?" she asked. "But it can wait until morning! To bed now, go on!"

Camilla fell asleep as soon as her head hit the pillow. Mephisto, who had rolled himself into a big tight ball, opened one eye as Camilla sank down beside him, then slumbered on. Lynn lay awake for a long time. Everything that had happened was playing like a movie through her head, one moment ghosts, and the next, thieves. It was all too much to deal with at once! So Arnold and Chatty Kathy were the ones slinking around in the wee hours…

But what did they want with those old letters? That was what Lynn didn't understand. Were they hoping to find a clue to the treasure? That could be, but... how could they find anything if Mephisto was sitting on top of the pile? No, now he was transformed into a kitten and getting tangled in spider webs...

Lynn fell into a deep, long sleep.

Chapter 12

Explanation

There were no signs of life on the top floor of the house until shortly before noon. Camilla woke up first.

"No! It can't be that late!" she exclaimed, looking at the clock in disbelief.

"What?" Lynn sat up sleepily in bed. She had just been dreaming that Mephisto was an enchanted frog and right before she woke up, he'd been jumping back and forth on the ground, croaking non-stop.

Lynn rubbed the sleep from her eyes and observed that Mephisto was his normal self. He was standing by the door meowing impatiently.

"Poor Mephisto! He's hungry." Camilla yawned as she opened the door for him to run to his breakfast.

"The horses!" cried Lynn, alarmed. "They must be starving. We've slept through half the day!"

The girls hurriedly got dressed and bounded down the stairs. When they got to the entry hall, Anne appeared.

"Good morning," she said, beaming. "I thought it must be you. It sounded like stampeding elephants up there. Come into the kitchen and have some breakfast, or shall we just call it lunch at this point?"

"We have to feed the horses first," answered Camilla.

"Don't worry! Thomas has already gone out there and given them enough water and hay to last a couple of days. Now, come on!" she said, practically shoving them into the kitchen.

Lynn was more interested in going out to the stable, but she was also curious about what had happened after she and Camilla had gone to bed.

∞∞∞

While the girls ate as if they hadn't had anything for weeks, Anne kept them company. She was still smiling and seemed in a very good mood. "There's so much to tell you, I don't know where to begin," she said. "But first of all, the two guests we unmasked last night were indeed the two who were sneaking around and stealing things. And it was Mr. Stevens who attacked me in the library."

"So it must have been Chatty K — Mrs. Andersen — who locked us up in the supply shed," said Camilla indignantly.

118

"That's right," said Anne. "But actually their names aren't Stevens or Andersen. They're married to each other and have a totally different last name. But she played the part of the dumb loudmouth, and he pretended he was sick of listening to her blab on all the time. I have to say it was good acting!"

The girls agreed. They would never have thought those two were working together.

"And by the way, their last name is Butler," Anne continued. "Sounds familiar, doesn't it?"

Lynn and Camilla gaped, open-mouthed. "Does that mean they're related to us?" Camilla asked.

"As it turns out, yes. He's a distant relative we didn't know existed." Anne shrugged. "But we're not exactly proud of his relation to us."

She picked up her coffee mug and then put it down before she'd taken another sip. "He spilled the whole story before the police took them away. He read about the treasure that was supposed to be here and decided to find it. Of course he's the one who stole the diary."

Anne looked at the book, which lay open on the kitchen table.

"And we thought it was Oliver Dale," said Lynn, shaking her head. "How stupid of us!"

"Well, he was acting pretty suspiciously too," said Camilla.

"Mr. Dale's an odd character," echoed Anne. "I have to admit I thought he was the one who attacked me. But I was wrong."

She reached out and picked up the diary.

"The diary made it clear that Elvira's cousin collected art objects and books. That's why Stevens – I'll still call

119

him that because I don't want to admit he's a Butler…" said Anne with a grimace. "Anyway, that's why he looked through all the paintings he'd seen here and all the art objects up in the attic and in the stable."

"So he took your painting down from the wall?" asked Lynn.

Anne nodded. "He thought I might have unknowingly painted over a masterpiece. But when he took it down and examined the back of the canvas, he realized that it was much too recent to have been bought by Elvira's cousin. Then he and his wife made a list of all the paintings down here and in the attic along with the names of the painters, and sent it to an art dealer asking if any of them might be valuable. The answer was in that letter that I gave to Eva Arnesen by mistake. Chatty Kathy as you call her, was very upset that a stranger could have read the answer and might have asked her what it was all about."

"Now I see why she made such as fuss about that letter," said Lynn, remembering the scene in the entry hall all over again.

"But the answer she got was a disappointment for her," Anne continued. "None of the artists was very famous, so all the trouble she and Stevens had gone to turned out to be for nothing."

"So that's when Mr. Stevens started looking through the books in the library," concluded Camilla, "and you came in and surprised him!"

"He said he was so panicked he couldn't think clearly. He just grabbed the first thing he saw and threw it over my head. I guess I should be thankful he didn't use the collected works of William Shakespeare," said Anne with a laugh. "Anyway, the books aren't really valuable either. A couple of them are worth something, but not a fortune."

"So he tried to find some more clues in the old letters," continued Camilla triumphantly.

"Not quite," Anne said with a radiant smile. "Those letters themselves are the treasure."

"Huh?" Camilla and Lynn didn't understand.

"Not the actual letters, but the postage stamps on the envelopes!" Anne shook her head as if she still couldn't believe it. "Stevens finally hit on it when he remembered Elvira's remark that her cousin was always bragging about his letters from England. It's incredible to think they were right here under our noses all the time, without any of us thinking about those dusty old pieces of paper being worth anything. Elvira's cousin must have been ahead of his time to understand that the stamps would be worth a fortune some day."

"And? Are they? I mean, worth a fortune?" Camilla gazed at her mother expectantly.

Anne nodded. "Thomas took them to a stamp dealer in town this morning to have them assessed. That could take a while. But one thing is for sure – we won't have any financial problems in the future. We can restore the place just like we were planning to, and run our cozy little hotel without worrying about every penny. It's just wonderful news!"

"Just imagine! If we had been any later, they could have gotten away with the whole fortune!" Thinking about it made Lynn dizzy. If she and Camilla hadn't come in right at that moment, then…

As if she could read their minds, Anne said, "It's

thanks to you that this has turned out so well. By the way, I'd love to know what you two saw in the stable last night."

When the girls had finished their story Anne admitted, "I just don't know what to think." Camilla had also told her about Elvira's letter, even though earlier she'd decided not to.

"I've always said that ghosts only exist in people's imaginations, but now I'm not so sure… you two saw one, I don't doubt it, and that disappearing letter is also pretty odd, but…"

Anne stared at the wall and thought a while. Suddenly she looked up and said, "I think I've had enough for now. We can talk more about it later. But you girls should get out to the stable. Thomas is there and has a surprise for you."

Camilla and Lynn were terribly curious, but Anne wasn't giving anything away.

∞∞◇∞∞

"Pinch me again! I must be dreaming!" exclaimed Lynn, overjoyed.

"No way!" laughed Camilla. "Or else your whole arm will be black and blue. I've pinched you four times now. You're awake, honest!"

"And I am too," said Thomas with a laugh. "I hope you like your reward for catching the criminals!"

"Do I!" Lynn threw her arms around her uncle's neck and then ran over to Falcon again. He raised his head as if to say, "All right, that's enough with the mush! Don't get carried away!"

122

"It's the best reward I could ever think of. You're really sure he's mine?"

"For the tenth time – YES!" Thomas confirmed. "Falcon is yours, that's for sure. Everything's been arranged, and your parents have agreed to it. He'll stay here until we can find a good stable near your home, and until then you can come visit him as often as you like."

Lynn could hardly comprehend it all. Just for catching Arnold Stevens at the right time, she'd gotten what she'd always wanted: a horse of her very own. And if that wasn't enough, Uncle Thomas and Aunt Anne were even going to cover all his expenses.

Thomas went back to the house. Camilla smiled as she watched Lynn, who kept on walking around Falcon and examining him from all angles, as if she were afraid he'd disappear in a puff of smoke if she stopped looking at him for a second.

"When you're done admiring him, maybe we could take a nice ride." Camilla motioned to the window with her head. "You might not have noticed, but the weather is beautiful outside."

"Oh, sure, I'd love to!" Lynn agreed. "I'll be ready in a minute. I just have to saddle up my horse."

My horse! The sound of the words! She and Falcon had a glorious afternoon ahead of them, and that was only the beginning. As Lynn went to get Falcon's saddle, she was whistling loudly from pure joy.

Chapter 13
United forever

It was late in the evening and a faint moon cast an eerie light over the woods. The two girls were crouched behind a few bushes at the edge of a small clearing.

"Are you sure this is the right place?" whispered Lynn, for at least the fifth time.

"Yessssssss, Miss High-strung!" answered Camilla. "Calm down!"

"You calm down yourself!" Lynn shot back.

"Shh," hissed Camilla. "I think I hear something!" She peered around in the darkness. But everything was still. They sat, waiting, for a long time.

Lynn jumped when the screech of an owl broke the silence. It was still pretty creepy out here in the dark, silent woods, but if Camilla really thought that…

The minutes passed without anything happening. Lynn was about to say she'd had enough waiting around, when Camilla grabbed her arm.

"Look at that!" she whispered excitedly.

Lynn watched… and felt the hairs on the back of her neck rising. A little farther away, between the trees, it wasn't dark any more. A shining blue light like the one they'd seen in the stable was floating towards the clearing. As it approached, its shape became clearer and Lynn could make out a tall young man dressed in 19th-century clothing. He stood in the clearing, searching with his eyes. For a second he seemed to look directly at the girls. Lynn held her breath. His gaze passed them by. A few seconds passed. Then from far away they heard a neigh.

Lynn let go of Camilla's hand. She was so excited she almost couldn't sit still. A moment later an unforgettable scene took place in front of them. A large, elegant horse appeared before the trees, carrying a beautiful young woman dressed in an old-fashioned riding costume.

The horse halted near the young man. For one breathless second everything stopped as the young lovers gazed at each other. Then he stepped over to the horse with a smile and helped the woman down. They stood in an intimate embrace for a long time before he helped her into the saddle again and nimbly got up behind her. The horse set off from the clearing and disappeared among the trees. Soon there was nothing but a faint blue light, and even that disappeared within a few heartbeats.

At last! After more than a hundred years Andrew and

Elvira were united, this time for good. And Lynn and Camilla had made it all possible.

Something white shone on the spot where the horse had stood. Camilla walked slowly over to it, picked it up, and looked at it.

"Elvira's letter!" she cried, surprised.

Carefully, she turned the paper over and gave a startled cry. Something was there that she hadn't seen before. A strong, masculine hand had written, "Thank you".

"Andrew must have known we'd come here," said Camilla softly, showing Lynn the letter. "He was hoping we'd find it."

The girls looked at each other. Both of them had tears in their eyes.

They stayed there for a while staring off into the dark woods. Then they walked slowly back home, to where their horses were waiting.